An Italian Treat

Lilith Mor-Gan

An Italian Treat
Lilith Mor-Gan

Senior Editors & Producers: Contento
Editing: Lindy Kawalsky
Book Design :Talma Asher
Cover Design: Benjie Herskowitz

ISBN: 978-965-550-555-9

International sole distributor: Contento
22 Isserles Street, 6701457 Tel Aviv, Israel
www.ContentoNow.com
Netanel@contento-publishing.com

An Italian Treat

Lilith Mor-Gan

Contents

Dina 1

Mirale 2

Eitan 3

Esther 4

Noa 5

Lital 6

Ronit 7

Ron-Lee 8

Sarah 9

Yisrael 10

Dina

Who doesn't love Dina? Her voice is as soft and soothing as a cool breeze on a hot summer's day and her warm smile lights up her green, cat-like eyes in a way that leaves nobody feeling indifferent. Her blond ponytail sways majestically with every nod of her head, while her slim figure fits neatly into a tight pair of jeans paired with a worn out T-shirt that somehow looks great on her. In short, everyone is enamored with her, especially the men on the Kibbutz, where she has lived since she was a child; but also the women, who have managed to overcome their envy of her beauty. The pupils in her fifth grade class adore her; the stray cats and abandoned dogs love her (especially on Tuesdays when she brings them the leftover chicken from the Kibbutz's kitchen); the flowers in her little garden feel well cared for; and even the caterpillars appreciate the few weeds she purposefully leaves for them. The anxious human resources manager, who is in charge of finding temporary replacements for sick or absent workers, calls her almost every night. The bitter-mouthed woman from the Laundromat delays her with long talks on the Kibbutz's walking pathway, laying out her complaints one by one. Even the sour-faced dentist who usually tells patients who come for first aid to "take an antibiotic and come back next week," is willing to see her without an appointment.

Everybody knows that if you need someone to organize a festive dinner for two hundred guests on the eve of a holiday, you go talk to Dina. If there is still no one to plan the wedding ceremony for Shulinka and Chocho two weeks before the scheduled date, you should really talk to Dina. And if you are desperately looking for a human resources manager who won't quarrel with half the members and give the other half the cold shoulder, then you must definitely talk to, Dina.

She always listens willingly, empathizing with everyone, regardless of whether he is the human resources manager or the person in charge of organizing the High Holiday ceremonies, and she always agrees to do whatever she can to help out. Sometimes when the tasks at hand accumulate to a worrying magnitude, a flicker of panic can be seen on her usually friendly face. When one of the Kibbutz members who holds a managerial position approaches her in an attempt to get something done, however, that flicker can easily be ignored.

Dina met Yisrael, her loving husband of the past fifteen years, when she came to the Kibbutz as a girl, shortly after her father committed suicide and it became evident that her sickly mother couldn't raise her on her own. Dina, who was well aware of her mother's frailness and her own cumbersome presence, tried very hard to diminish herself and her physical needs to a state of almost non-existence, and she almost succeeded until she met Bilha, the caretaker at the Kibbutz. At the time, Dina was twelve years old, a scrawny girl with big green eyes and protruding bones. She knew she had to make people like her if she wanted to survive.

Bilha took one worried look at her and went straight to the general secretary of the Kibbutz. She was determined to bang on his door until she got Dina an appointment with the psychologist at the Family Health Care Center, and she wasn't going to take no for an answer. The secretary tried to convince Bilha that he didn't have a budget for therapy, particularly for a girl who was not a daughter of a member of the Kibbutz and only in temporary custody there. But after a heated debate, even he realized he was fighting a losing battle and agreed to six months' worth of therapy sessions for Dina. To Bilha's grave disappointment, Dina refused to go. She told Bilha she just didn't feel she needed to. What she failed to mention, however, was that things in the children's home had already become difficult for her with the other children calling her "Skeleton," and she was certainly not going to give them a reason to call her "Crazy" as well. The potential for more severe name calling was buzzing around in Dina's head. The last thing she wanted was to be known as "The Crazy Skeleton."

As time passed, Dina settled in with her adopted family on the Kibbutz. She felt mostly at home in Rina and Doron's apartment where she spent the afternoons, between four and seven, with their other four children before going back to the children's home for the night. She saw her sickly mother a few times a year, mostly on holidays, but frankly she didn't miss her very much. The Kibbutz had become her family and home and she couldn't imagine having another.

Yisrael, who also grew up on the Kibbutz as a boy from the "outside," had eight brothers and sisters. Dina was never sure if she had met them all because they were scattered all over the country in different boarding schools and Kibbutzim. This happened shortly after his father was sent to prison and his unemployed mother could no longer take care of the big family on her own. Every now and then Yisrael would mention with feigned indifference that his second oldest brother or his third youngest sister was supposed to come for a visit. Some degree of tension accompanied the expectation of criticism from them on the Kibbutz and the Kibbutz way of life that was certain to ensue from these visits, but since the visits were few, with many years in between, they never bothered Dina much.

Their mutual plight as "outsiders" had created a strong bond between Dina and Yisrael and by the eighth grade they had already officially become a couple. All the teachers knew that they always sat together at the first table by the window. By the end of the twelfth grade they were chosen as the couple of the year, and everybody knew that Dina and Yisrael would get married right after their army service, which of course they did.

Even after three pregnancies, Dina's figure is still slim and youthful. If it weren't for Yisrael's burning jealousy, many men would ask her to dance the couple dances at the folk dancing parties. Dina doesn't protest against Yisrael's unequivocal decree – no male dance partners. She accepts her husband's jealousy as a compliment and is satisfied in the arms of her best friend Mirale, who swirls her around in a fast polka.

Only late at night after putting the children to sleep, waking Yisrael, who usually falls asleep in front of the TV, and sending him to the bedroom, does she sit down at the small dining table in a circle of light to go over her task list. Organizing the holidays at the Kibbutz involves many people and requires meticulous preparation in order to run smoothly. Who has already finished doing what she asked him to do for the coming holiday eve, and who still needs constant reminders? Who should be approached about the special seating arrangements? Which songs should be chosen for the singing before dinner is served? Who can she ask to lead the singing without risking an immediate refusal? When she feels her eyes closing in spite of her efforts to keep them open, she gets up with a deep sigh and stretches until she hears her joints crack.

Quickly and efficiently she goes through her daily ritual in front of the mirror on the little cabinet, above the white sink. Flossing, brushing for three minutes, not too hard so as to not wear down her gums, as the dentist has instructed her, gargling mouth wash, facial cleansing, night cream, eye and neck cream, also applied in the cleavage area where the skin is thin and can easily get wrinkled. Most of the time she sleeps on her back, having started this habit after noticing that sleeping on her side made the wrinkles in her cleavage grow alarmingly deeper. She takes the foot and hand lotion to bed so she doesn't have to walk with greasy feet on the not-so-clean floor.

By the time she lifts the end of the blanket carefully and nestles herself slowly into the space beside him,

Yisrael is sound asleep. When her head touches the pillow, she feels his hands reaching for her, groping for her breasts. She holds her breath. Maybe this time fatigue will overcome him and he will fall asleep again, but his aimless caresses become more and more focused and now he is holding her left breast in his hand, massaging it lightly. She sighs quietly and weighs her options: if she declines his wordless offer, she will have to pay the penalty the next morning. His sulking silent treatment will require a lot of apologizing and sucking up (maybe even literally) to make him snap out of it. On the other hand, if she can find the energy, she will get it over and done within a few minutes and maybe even manage to enjoy herself a little in the process.

After a moment's hesitation she turns to him and kisses his neck. He acknowledges her acceptance by enthusiastically lifting her night gown and, with his eyes still closed, takes off her panties. She lifts his T-shirt and presses her naked breasts to his warm hairy chest, moving them from side to side. She likes the way his chest hair tickles her breasts. He spreads her legs and gently inserts his finger into her barely moist slit while his thumb is rubbing her tiny love button. The combined motion produces sighs of pleasure that come from her half open mouth. She starts moving her pelvis against his fingers, but before she can savor the gentle, tantalizing touch, he rolls onto her and with one skilled movement inserts his engorged organ into her. She gives up on the immediate clitoral orgasm and raises her pelvis to him, helping him thrust deeper into her. She likes feeling him deep, deep inside her, almost on the verge of causing pain. She moves her hips in a rhythm synchronized to his movements, clenching and relaxing her muscles alternately, a technique she remembers the sex therapist explaining to them in the riveting lecture a few months before.

Yisrael picks up the pace. Still in a state of foggy drowsiness, he forgets to do what she has repeatedly asked him to do, to probe with his forefinger into her anus. Dina bites her lower lip, hesitant about whether to remind him or not. She longs for that feeling of double penetration, which invariably lifts her towards the desired culmination of sexual excitement, but she doesn't want to distract him, so she tries to clear her head of all other thoughts and concentrate on the sweeping rhythm. She knows she doesn't have long before he will come. If she wants to have her orgasm as well, she must concentrate. It is probably Yisrael's drowsiness that enables her to ride the tidal wave and come just a second before his face contorts. He pushes his organ into her one last time and collapses on top of her.

"Be a doll and bring me something to wipe up with," he asks her in a sleepy voice, but when she comes back with toilet paper and wet wipes he is already breathing the deep, calm breath of sleep. She smiles tiredly, leans over and wipes his organ, which lies flaccid and vulnerable in the palm of her hand, like a fledgling fallen from the nest.

The morning comes as always, much too early. Dina sighs and forces herself to move her feet out from under the warm blanket and down on to the cold tiles. The morning schedule is very tight and any deviation from it leads to her and Alon missing the school bus. She shakes Yisrael's shoulder and impatiently watches him sit up slowly in bed, yawing and stretching his arms. They work together with great agility, like a well-trained crew. He makes sandwiches while she wakes up Dana and Keren. She washes their faces and dresses them. Alon, a second grade pupil, is already independent and doesn't need her help to get ready, except for a reminder to put his science project in his school bag and take his sandwich and water bottle. At a quarter past seven Dina takes Dana to the nursery while Yisrael drops Keren at Kindergarten. At half past seven she and Alon are already on their way to school. Dina tries to remember to not caress his head absent-mindedly and to not call him "Alonush" within hearing range of his friends, an act that will make him sulk all day and avoid interacting with her at school. She sits down in her regular seat beside Mirale and exhales a sigh of relief, finally allowing herself to relax from the stress of the morning routine.

"Don't forget tonight's lecture," Dina says. "I heard the lecturer is an amazing woman, and remind Shosh to come as well."

"What's it about anyway?" Mirale asks with a wide yawn.

"It's called 'A Guided Mediation,' but it's not as boring as it sounds," Dina promises her. "She also uses tarot cards and all sorts of mystical things. It should be interesting enough to make all those lazy Kibbutz members abandon their TV sets for an hour and come to a social gathering in the Members' Club," Dina adds sourly.

In spite of the widespread publicity for the "Mystical Evening," only a handful of Kibbutz members show up at the club. Dina sighs. She wonders what it will take to get the members out of the comfort of their homes. A striptease show, perhaps, no less than that. The lecturer, a pretty woman in her thirties, feels Dina's distress and consoles her. "It's better to have a small group of people who are really into it than a big group of loud-mouthed skeptics. You'll see, we'll have a great time." Dina doesn't feel encouraged yet, but it is difficult not to respond to the woman's radiant smile.

The lecturer talks about "the inner child," the care-free and fun-loving aspect of our souls that we repress and ignore in order to function in the serious grown-ups' world. "So gradually we abandon the inner child in us, who also needs loving attention," she says softly, "that child who likes to laugh and play, who is constantly inventing new things just for the fun of it, that child who experiences life as an ongoing amazing adventure, and not as a series of duties, hardships and sufferings that we have to endure. We have all learned how to be responsible adults ["Not ALL of us," Eitan whispers cynically, but is quickly hushed up by Mirale], and we have been living so long according to the rules and norms of the grown-ups' world that we have forgotten how to listen to that child. We have gradually lost our ability to play. We need to get in touch with our inner child so it can teach us how to once again find joy in the things we do. We need to find that child in us to show us how to have fun again."

Dina feels every word sinking in, creating an inexplicable internal tremor in her. Although, seemingly, there is nothing new in what the lecturer is saying, nothing that she hasn't read before in the New Age books she has started taking an interest in recently, somehow the lecturer's soft, warm voice gives it more validity and urgency. After the lecture they practice guided meditation. They lie on mattresses in the darkened room watching candlelight dance on the ceiling. Dina feels how the soft music unwinds the tension in her shoulders and disperses her usual train of thought, like smoke in the wind. She inhales deeply through her nose and exhales slowly through her o-shaped lips until a tingling sensation spreads over her whole body and a strange lightness overtakes her.

The lecturer instructs them to imagine they're going for a walk in a beautiful place, on the way they meet their inner child. Dina hesitates for a minute, and then her thoughts carry her back to Gordon beach of Tel-Aviv. That was the only place she could go to as a child to escape the busy, suffocating urban environment. She used to spend the long hot days of summer on the beach with her friends. Swimming in the warm water, playing volleyball on the sand and just lying there reading books and chatting until they became as tanned as the beautiful Tahitians on the calendar that used to hang in her father's workshop, before he went bankrupt.

Dina visualizes herself walking on the beach very much like Gordon beach, only there is nobody there except her; golden sands, lightly kissed by foaming waves, stretch as far as the eye can see. The crystal blue water and blue sky have infinity between them. From afar she sees a small figure playing in the sand. She quickens her steps and when she gets closer she notices it's a little girl in a pink bikini with blue flowers, just like the one she used to have. The girl is absorbed in cupping wet sand in her tiny hands and letting it drip through her fingers, creating complex stalagmites on her sand castle. She kneels by the little girl and caresses her hair.

"Hi sweetheart," she says gently.

The child lifts her head and gives her a small smile, but deep sadness lurks in her emerald eyes.

"What are you doing?" Dina asks, sitting down beside her.

The girl doesn't answer and tries to hide her face.

"Are you angry with me?" She phrases it as a question although she knows the answer.

"So you finally came," says the girl in a perturbed voice. "I had almost given up on you. I thought you'd never come again."

Dina feels her heart going out to the disappointed child. "Oh no," she coos, as though comforting one of her own children, "I'd never leave you."

"Yeah, that's what you said the last time you came to visit, but that was such a long time ago, I've even forgotten when it was." The girl speaks with a bitterness that doesn't become her young age. Suddenly she turns to Dina and asks her directly. "Why have you forgotten about me?"

Dina lowers her head. "I really don't know what to tell you… you know how life goes on… and the routine schedule is so tight and demanding. Everybody wants a piece of me – my children, my husband, my pupils, my Kibbutz – they all need things, want things from me, and I keep running around, trying to do the best I can in the best way possible. I know I don't always succeed, but at least I try to do the best I can."

The girl pouts and stares angrily at her. "That's just a grown-up excuse. I knew you'd make up something like that. I don't even know why I bothered asking…"

Dina is silent for a minute. The girl lifts her plastic spade and starts demolishing her sand castle. "I'm sorry." Dina's voice is half choked. The girl keeps pounding down the stalagmites. "Did you hear what I said? I AM sorry." Dina raises her voice, determined to win back the girl's trust.

"If you're really sorry, don't talk so much. Show me how sorry you are," the girl blurts out without even looking at her.

Dina is embarrassed. She hesitates for a moment, then spreads her arms and hugs the girl. She cradles her on her lap and whispers in her ear, "I'm sorry, darling, I'm really so very, very sorry I've abandoned you for such a long, long time." The girl's body is stiff at first but she quickly melts in Dina's arms, returning the hug. They remain in their embrace for a while, moving gently together like seaweed in the currents. "What would you like me to do for you?" Dina whispers.

The girl ponders the question for a moment. "I don't know, just think of me every now and then and come visit me, and do things with me like we used to – playing in the sand, looking for sea shells, laughing and dancing, but *my* dances, the ones *I* make up, not your boring folk dancing. Just don't forget about me."

"I promise." Dina knows this is one promise she mustn't break.

On the way home Mirale chatters excitedly about the things she has experienced, what the lecturer said to her, what she told Shosh, and how Shosh had her head in the clouds and felt she was floating (those were her exact words), and how Shmil couldn't believe it when the lecturer told him about the little boy in the snow. He thought maybe Shosh told the speaker about him. After all, he had never revealed that story to anyone except for Shosh, so how the hell could the speaker have known about it? Dina is silent most of the time and just nods absentmindedly.

During the closing sharing circle, she had chosen not to tell her story of the meeting with the little girl on the beach. She felt it was too private, too powerful, to share with Shmil and Eitan who would probably tell it to all the factory workers during their coffee break the next day; or with Shosh who would make sure all the girls in the accountancy department knew all the details. From there it would spread to the kitchen workers, the Laundromat staff, the people at the clothing storeroom and the child caretakers, who would most likely be updated when they came to pick up lunch for the Kindergarten and nurseries. While half listening to Mirale, her thoughts wander once again to the sad little girl on the beach and the promise she has made her. Even when Yisrael asks her how the lecture was she can't bring herself to tell him the story, although she is usually glad when he takes an interest in what she does.

The days following that evening bring slight, almost imperceptible changes in Dina's behavior. She doesn't cut her hair short like she wants to because she knows Yisrael will be very upset if she does. Instead she dyes her hair a beautiful shade of reddish blond and asks the hair dresser to cut the ends so it will look a bit roughed up and wild, like the singers on MTV. She doesn't buy the pair of jeans that wrap her ass so appealingly because Alon wants new clothes with a print that all the other boys in his class have, and Keren wants a new dress for her birthday. But when she returns home and opens her wardrobe, she bites her lower lip, frowning, then removes all the buttoned up blouses that make her look like an old-fashioned teacher, folds them carefully and packs them in a parcel to be given to charity. She continues to say yes to everything that is asked of her. However when Shmil comes to tell her that his family from Netanya is coming for a visit for Tu Be-Shvat, and they are looking forward to the traditional ceremony of the planting of the trees, she tells him in an assertive voice that if he wants a tree-planting ceremony he should start arranging one. She cannot promise anything, especially now, with just a week left until the holiday and no volunteers for the holiday staff yet.

She doesn't say, nor does she do, anything out of the ordinary, but there is definitely something different about her, something that makes Keren, who usually enjoys arguing with her parents about bedtime, agree to go to bed quite easily on condition that Mummy tells her the story 'There's a Nightmare in my Closet' with all the appropriate spooky voices of the monsters. Even Dana, who usually only falls asleep with Mummy by her side caressing her hair, is satisfied with just half an hour of caressing while Mummy tells Keren the story, and then agrees to stay in bed as long as Mummy stays in the living room and the Snoopy night light is on. These negotiations take place every night, except for Monday evenings when the children are allowed to watch TV with Daddy until they fall asleep in front of it, while Mummy is in her weekly guided meditation meeting.

The romantic weekend in Rome, which she has dreamt about for so long, has finally become feasible. Things are working out better than she has dared to hope. Yisrael fights for them on all fronts. He stands up to Tzipi, the school principal, who frowns at the vacation request and says wryly that the Ministry of Education doesn't permit teachers to take vacations in the middle of the school year. He beseeches Netta, their regular babysitter, who doesn't like the idea of being stuck with the children for a whole weekend, to reconsider. Finally, he stands up to the factory manager who claims he just can't manage without Yisrael for a whole weekend. Dina can't believe they are actually going until the airplane takes off and she sees Tel-Aviv getting smaller and smaller beneath the airplane wing and finally fading away into the blue horizon.

The weather in Rome isn't very welcoming. Chilly wind greets them when they exit the plane, but Dina breathes it in joyously and trembles a little with excitement. The next day the sun comes out intermittently through the grey, threatening clouds, and they go to all the sites that Dina has carefully marked in the guidebook she's holding. She can hardly contain herself. She wants to run from site to site and jump with excitement at finally seeing the famous sites she has read about and seen in so many movies— Forum Romanum, the Colloseum and the Pantheon. She drags Yisrael behind her while reading from the guidebook until her feet are tired and she declares they deserve to rest in one of the lovely little cafés on the piazza.

The next day is rainy and they decide to pamper themselves with a more relaxed day that includes a big breakfast and a walk down the cobblestone streets with no special destination. Maybe it is the cool air, spotted with misty rain droplets, the pink and white cyclamens along Via Veneto or the romantic charm of Fontana di Trevi with its larger than life marble figures overlooking the fountain pool; or maybe it is something entirely different that stirs Dina's heart, producing uncharacteristic playfulness. While walking down Via Veneto they are enthralled with the European-style majestic appearance of the doormen at the entrances to the various hotels. Their fancy formal uniforms make them look like they belong there, and not like they are dressed in costumes for a Purim party.

Suddenly it starts raining. Dina squeaks with pleasure and they start running in the rain, holding hands and laughing. They can't go into any of the fancy hotels so they enter a book caravan that is parked on the street corner. They wander around looking at the books that are stacked from floor to ceiling. Yisrael is leafing through some travel guides and Dina is looking for art books, when she notices a big book with a very interesting picture on the cover. She opens the cover and becomes so absorbed in it that she doesn't hear Yisrael sneaking up behind her until she is startled by his voice.

"What is this book that has caught your full attention?"

Dina blushes, closes the book quickly and hides it behind her back. This only serves to arouse Yisrael's curiosity and he playfully wrestles with her to pry the book from her hands. Finally, she yields and hands the book over, sneaking a worried look to see his reaction. The picture on the cover, a handsome, smiling, bare-chested man on the background of a golden wheat field, doesn't prepare Yisrael for how that same man and others, are shown inside the book. The book is filled with naked men on backgrounds of wild countryside scenes, proudly flaunting their sky high erections and exposing their tight masculine asses to the camera. These are rough, virile men whose sweat you can almost smell. Dina nervously watches the surprised lift of Yisrael's left brow and the amused look on his face as he flips the pages. He lets out a low whistle.

"So… this is what has kept you riveted," he says in an undecipherable tone.

She nods, not daring to take her eyes off him.

"I never thought of you as the kind of girl who would be interested in pictures of … this kind."

Does she hear a tone of reproach in his voice? Should she say she was interested to see what IT looked like on other men, but now that she has satisfied her curiosity she isn't interested anymore? Can she hide the quickening of her pulse when she looks at these naked men?

He closes the book and looks at her with a smile she can't exactly interpret. "It has turned you on, this book. Admit it."

She exhales with relief, gives him a long look and nods slightly. A little smile starts showing at the corner of her mouth.

To her great surprise, he takes her hand and says with resolution, "I'm buying you this book. It's my special gift to you, from Rome."

Yisrael insists that they take a taxi back to the hotel. Luckily the driver doesn't seem interested in what is going on in the back seat. Yisrael looks at Dina like a teenager in love. He drapes his arm around her, pulling her closer to him. She buries her face in his chest, inhaling his familiar scent. The hairs on his chest that come out through his unbuttoned shirt tickle her nose. He smells like home, like a steady anchor, like masculine pheromones. He starts kissing her face, her forehead, and then slowly traces her jaw line with his soft lips, down to her ear lobes, where he takes his time exploring every crease and niche of her ears. "You're so beautiful, my lovely, lovely wife," he murmurs in her ear as his hot breath sends little shudders of pleasure down her spine. She pulls his shirt out from his jeans and tucks her hand under his vest. She loves running her fingers through the hair on his chest. She starts playing with his nipples, caressing, pinching, pulling them gently, and he moans with pleasure. She knows the effect this has on him and smiles secretly. He retaliates by descending to that wonderfully sensuous spot in the crevice of her neck, where he sucks and nibbles her silky skin until her knees start to quiver. This is *her* hot spot and he's a smooth operator. He is perfectly willing to go lower but she somehow summons the strength to stop him with a silent, amused reproach. The moments in the taxi are prolonged by the charged expectation that trembles between them. Every traffic light is a sweet torture; their bodies cry out for each other, emitting coded signals of scent and longing. Waiting to become united in passionate lovemaking becomes almost unbearable.

When they finally arrive at their room in the hotel, Yisrael is so eager to get Dina into bed that he starts undressing her at the door, but to his utter surprise she pushes him onto the bed and says in a commanding voice that holds but a hint of laughter, "No. This time you're going to watch. Just watch."

Surprised, he obeys this new voice of hers, feeling a little insulted, but at the same time also terribly aroused. She turns on the TV set and puts it on the MTV channel. The rhythmic melody of one of the latest hits is heard and Dina starts dancing, a little hesitantly at first, but soon her muscles tune in and her movements become more and more serpentine as she claims the space of the whole room. Her eyes are closed as she arches her back and moves her pelvis in slow, enticing circles. Yisrael gazes at her as if he is seeing her for the first time in his life. She extends one arm, then the other, crossing them over her hips, while moving sinuously to the beat. She lifts her shirt slowly above her head. Now she's dancing in her bra and jeans, and her smooth skin glistens in the soft light. She turns around so her back is to him and slowly unhooks her bra, which she then tauntingly throws at him. She turns around, her hands cupping her small round breasts and rubbing her pink nipples with her thumbs. Yisrael's breath catches. He reaches to his jeans, opens the belt and the zipper and sets his erection free. He watches her intently as she puts one finger into her mouth and moistens her nipples, taking pleasure in feeling them hardening.

She opens her eyes to see Yisrael looking at her, his gaze so intense it almost incinerates her. She smiles a little smile, content that her scheme is working, and continues dancing. She takes her hands off her breasts, setting them free, letting them bounce joyously with her every movement. She reaches for her ponytail, pulls out the band and lifts her hair, wrapping it around her face and bare breasts, peering from behind its shimmering veil to see the effect her actions are having on Yisrael. His breath becomes short and rapid. Smiling a secret little smile, she starts caressing herself, making little circles around her tits, and then floating her fingertips over her belly. With very slow movements, excruciatingly slowly, she unzips her jeans and starts sliding them down while still gyrating to the sound of the music. At last she stands before him with just her lace panties on, moving her finger over the rise of her pubic hair which can be seen through the thin lace. Yisrael can't stand the accumulating tension any more. He gets up to hug her, but she assertively puts her hand on his chest and pushes him back onto the bed, saying in a mock command, "I told you that you're only watching now!"

Astonished at the mischievous glint in her eye, which is so new to him, he lies down again, not taking his eyes off her for a minute. He doesn't know where it's all going, but the new Dina is so charming and adorable that he is willing to do as she bids him. Dina goes on dancing, her hands floating over her breasts, her belly and the sensitive skin on the insides of her thighs. Her eyes are closed as if she gazing inside herself, into that shaded place whose description eludes her, a place she once visited but whose location has gotten lost due to all her daily obligations and responsibilities. Her right hand sweeps down her belly and finds its way under the fine fabric of her panties. Yisrael holds his breath. Her hand starts moving, her knuckles visible through the white lace.

"Take off your panties," he begs her, his voice husky with passion.

Without opening her eyes and without taking her right hand out from its hiding place, she pushes her panties down until they reach her ankles and are cast aside in one graceful movement. She stands naked before him, her glorious body still moving with the rhythm. He extends his arms to welcome her to his embrace, but to his surprise she walks to the armchair by the window and sits down, her legs spread wide. Yisrael has a clear view of her flower of paradise, which opens its bright pink petals for him. Her fingers keep on playing with her pleasure button, circling it, slapping it lightly, occasionally descending into her glistening crevice. Absorbed in pleasuring herself, her face is serious and focused. Yisrael wets his hand and starts sliding it up and down his erect member in a slow motion, unconsciously timing himself with her movements. Her fingers move faster and faster until short wailing sounds come from her parted lips, like the cries of a distant bird. Her whole body trembles and then convulses as the orgasm seizes her. She bends forward and then immediately arches her body backward, her ass in the air, and the pent-up cry that has been accumulating in her lithe body bursts forth into the air, bouncing off the room's walls like the primordial cry of a newborn.

Yisrael hurries to her, taking her spent body in his arms as if she were a little girl. She melts in his arms, her eyes closed and her face serene. He puts her on the bed and looks at her, admiring every delectable curve of her body. She radiates warmth and light as from an inner furnace. He covers her with soft kisses – her eyes, her lips, her neck, trailing kisses down the path between her breasts and that almost invisible path of fair hair that leads from her naval to her hill of pleasures. She draws a deep breath when he hovers with his mouth just above her open lotus flower. She can feel his scorching breath on her outer lips and she groans, spreading her legs wider, but he doesn't succumb to temptation just yet. He climbs up again, all the way to that dimple in her neck, which, when nibbled, makes her squirm under him.

"You took your time playing with me," he whispers huskily. "Now it's my turn." Making his way down again, he circles her apple-like breasts with his tongue. Slowly he closes in on her rosy nipples, teasing them with the tip of his tongue. Then, taking the whole nipple in his mouth, he sucks it gently while he plays with her other nipple with his free hand. The unmistakable odor of her awakening passion envelops him in a stupefying cloud of passion that makes him want to dedicate his life to satisfying her desires. He kisses her soft, warm belly, this time dedicating more attention to the sensitive spots along her hips. Dina feels a light tingling sensation growing in her body with every passing second. She longs for him to finish his journey down her body and reach her vibrating, steaming cave. He notices her impatience and smiles to himself as he deliberately avoids passing through the apex of her thighs, instead detouring around it and descending to trail his lips along the inner sides of her thighs and the sensitive skin behind her knees. She groans loudly, writhing under him, begging him, "Eat me, eat me now." Finally he goes back to the center of her being, separates her vibrating inner lips to reveal her quivering, fuchsia pink inner sanctum. When she feels his hot, eager tongue licking her thoroughly, Dina feels the tingling sensation grow into an inner tremor that threatens to shatter her to pieces. He starts sucking on her love button while his index finger is drilling into her love canal, looking for that elusive little spot that feels slightly rougher than the smooth walls. When he finds it, he starts rubbing it at the same time his thumb is rubbing her love button and his tongue is licking her all over.

Dina feels her consciousness melting into that hot spot in the center of her being, carried by pulsating waves of sensation that spread through her body like ripples in a pond. The waves grow taller and more powerful as she lets herself be carried away to a place she's never been before. This is it, she thinks, it can't get any better than this. But at that moment she feels another route of deep pleasure opening up in her body as Yisrael's finger finds her anus and slides inside it with rotating movements. The double pressure reverberates in her nerves, sending tingling electrical sensations down to her toes and all the way up to the top of her head at the same time. She no longer knows who she is or what she is made of, except for that quivering mass of pure pleasure exploding in his arms. Suddenly his fingers disappear and she feels his erect organ probing her, as if knocking on the door to her castle, begging to be let in.

Succumbing to its mute plea, she softens and opens up to it, feeling it sliding eagerly inside her, filling her up. She is flooded with electric currents that emanate from the point where they are merged together. A huge tidal wave of sensations swooshes over her, lifting her up uncontrollably. Her body shakes, quivers and hums like a high voltage electricity pole. She feels his body echoing her convulsions with the tremendous burst of energy that he releases inside her. Her conscious mind evaporates and she feels herself immersed in this magnificent world where their combined bodies can conjure up magic the likes of which she has never experienced before. There is a deep, serene happiness in that release of corporal boundaries, in that yielding to the sweet pleasure that vibrates in the core of things.

They remain in their embrace for a long time, both shaken by the magnitude of the experience. When she feels Yisrael trying to roll off of her, she presses her legs around him and doesn't let him pull out of her.

"Let's stay like this a little longer," she whispers to him, caressing his sweaty forehead. She feels his weight as a calming pressure on her body. Their hearts beat together in a synchronized rhythm that sends wavelets of love back and forth between them.

Mirale

To Dina's disappointment, Mirale, her best friend, refuses to look at the book she brought from Rome. How could she tell her all the amazing stories of their adventures in Rome, stories that are all somehow tied to this book? The book had become the center of a magical maze, and everything she had gone through in her life seemed to either move toward it or away from it. Mirale just smiles when Dina brings up these arguments, but still obstinately refuses to look at "pictures unfit for a lady."

Neither her friend's entreaties, nor all the history of art that is enlisted to demonstrate the beauty of the naked human body, manage to persuade Mirale otherwise. Dina lectures her fervently on how, throughout the history of humankind, the beauty of the body has been celebrated, sculpted, painted, sung to, and written about. "Look at Botticelli's *Venus*, being born from the sea—the embodiment of female beauty."

"Personally, I never thought much of her horse face," Mirale mumbles.

"Then think about Renoir with his voluptuous, bathing women," Dina presses on.

"Sure, with all the folds of fat they have in their bellies they should participate in the TV show, *The Biggest Loser*," Mirale remarks cynically.

"And what about Gauguin, who revealed the beauty of the Tahitian women to the world? Can you deny the beauty of their bare breasts that rivals the lusciousness of ripe fruit on a platter?" Dina asks rhetorically.

"Yes, taking a fourteen-year-old girl for a wife after ditching his own wife and children in Paris… that's your role model?" Mirale replies sarcastically. Dina almost gives up on her obstinate friend.

"Really, I can't understand you. A beautiful body is one of God's most extraordinary gifts to us. You should have seen the female visitors to the Academy of Arts in Florence, especially the American ones. They ogled the statue of David admiringly, giggling as they walk around it, sighing like teenagers in love with a rock star. You would have to have been there under those almost-five meters of smooth, milky white marble carved into the most handsome man you've ever seen, in order to understand the feeling. His abs melt your knees, those broad shoulders are just calling to you to rest your head against them, and you know you want to be caressed by those gentle but very masculine hands with those prominent veins . . ." Dina sighs softly with the memory.

Suddenly her anger with her sanctimonious friend rises hotly. "What is unfitting here? Tell me! Admiring a beautiful body is admiring the beauty of God's creation; it's just like... praying!" Mirale raises an eyebrow at her friend's unusual outcry and moves uncomfortably in her chair. Her thoughts drift back to her teenage years.

"Close your legs, *mein kind*," her grandmother reprimands her sharply. "A lady never sits with her legs spread apart."

"But Granny," protests the fifteen-year-old Mirale. "I could understand that if I was wearing a dress, but in case you haven't noticed, I'm wearing a pair of thick jeans! What could people possibly see if I spread my legs, the seams of my jeans?"

Confronted with this light cynical arrow that has been shot in her direction, Mirale's grandmother makes an evasive maneuver. "A lady is always a lady," she reiterates. "It doesn't matter whether she's in rags or an evening gown. Don't forget that your grandfather came to the Levant because he was a Zionist. There was only sand here as far as the eye could see, no streets, no cars, no beautiful

Bauhaus buildings. Just sand. That and the Arabs. This was the Levant when we first came here, but it doesn't mean that you have to become a Levantine in order to live here! It is possible to maintain the heritage of your forefathers and still be a loyal Zionist. *Noblesse oblige* – do you know what it is? It means that anywhere and anytime in your life you *will* behave like my granddaughter. Your forefathers come from a very good family in Köln, and you will always think before you act. "

So, at the age of fifteen, Mirale started her life-long battle with the curse her grandmother had cast on her, "to always be the perfect lady." Her beautiful grandmother always had her hair done up in a spectacular snowy curve and her make-up delicately applied. Looking immaculate in her gray woolen suit and the pearl necklace and the diamond ring that Grandpa bought her for their golden anniversary, her loving grandmother had no idea of the nature of the hardships she had placed on her granddaughter, who had grown up in the Socialist society of Israel in the sixties and seventies. Mirale had never dared to do any of the things the other girls were doing, like dancing freely, moving their arms and swaying their hips, flirting with the boys, kissing at the slow dances when the room was darkened so the couples would feel free to do whatever they wanted. Mirale usually sat on a chair in the corner, too afraid to move, listening to the shuffle of feet and the sucking noises around her.

At the age of eighteen, on the Kibbutz with her Gari'in (a close group of boys and girls who went through the army together, hopefully to settle on a Kibbutz after their army service), just a few months before they were drafted to the army, Mirale felt as if she had been watching life through a glass window. There was an ambience of sexual tension and excitement around her. The girls who worked in the orchard talked about sneaking secret looks at the boys who took off their shirts because of the heat, and comparing the size of their biceps. Rumors circulated about nocturnal swims in the Kibbutz's pool, which didn't require the use of a bathing suit. The night watchmen whispered in the ears of their confidants at the breakfast table the latest news about who went into a room that wasn't his (or her) own, and at what hour of the late night or early morning he (or she) came out. But Mirale, still a virgin, didn't dare partake of these exhilarating events. She prided herself for not being air-headed and frivolous like the other girls, but deep in her heart she envied them bitterly.

One warm, lazy afternoon, all the girls lay on the lawn in a big noisy group, full of little giggles and squeaks that got louder and became stifled screams of pleasure when Noa started telling one of her conquest stories.

Mirale loathed that smug voice Noa used to tell about the night she had spent in the Canadian volunteer's bed. "Randy, girls. You know, his name says it all," said Noa smugly. "He's as horny as an off-shore sailor. Three times was not enough for him. These uncircumcised men, I'm telling you, they have something that we poor Jewish girls, who are condemned to lie with only Jewish men, will never experience. Let's admit it. We belong to the Jewish nation that tampers with one of God's most wonderful inventions, the male penis, in a misguided procedure and a seriously misconstrued perception of the functionality of the foreskin. So my testimony will probably remain uncorroborated, but nonetheless convincing I hope. An uncircumcised dick does something to you inside that no Jewish dick can ever do."

The high decibels that erupted from the gaggle of girls on the lawn attracted the attention of Tony, the American volunteer, and he came out of his room to join them. Hidden behind Dina's back, Mirale curiously spied on him. He had wanton, provocative beauty. His long blond curls rested on smooth, tanned, broad shoulders. His blue eyes regarded the girls with an unmistakable searching demeanor, while his tongue licked his strawberry-colored lips, and then his white teeth, very slowly. He bit slightly into his lower lip. Mirale found herself wondering how a man could possess such full red lips. If Tony had ever had any inhibitions, they were certainly not present when he dove into the pile of girls like a rock star jumping into his cheering audience. For a moment he was swallowed up in a whirlpool of hands, breasts, bellies, and long strands of hair that streamed over his half-naked body like seaweed. The next moment he floated up, his face aglow with exhilaration. The girls passed him from one to the other and he willingly succumbed to their charms, making the same offer to each one in turn. "Let me make love to you…"

Some of the girls played with him a little before passing him on, caressing his long curls and his smooth, hairless chest, which was so unlike the hairy chests of the other men on the Kibbutz. But they all refused his kind offer with a knowing smile, for Tony was a notorious sex-addict. The few girls who had taken up the challenge of trying to tame him hadn't lasted more than a week. Even when they reprimanded him for his intransigent disloyalty and his never-ending flirtations, he just looked at them with his puppy dog eyes and give them an innocent, melting look. All they could do was laugh and pass him on to the next girl who wanted to have a bit of fun.

In his defense, one must say that despite all of his faults, Tony was never deceitful. He never for a moment hid his intentions under beguiling but dishonest promises of love like the other boys did. He was transparently honest to the point of public embarrassment and never pretended to be what he was not. His philosophy of life was a simple one: live for the moment, preferably with a bottle of cold beer in your hand and get as much nuki-nuki as you possibly can. That was his favorite phrase. Mirale had to admit it sounded much better and more acceptable than "fucking."

When Tony was thrown into Mirale's lap, he smiled, extended his arm, cupped her head, and whispered in her ear, "Wanna lose your virginity to me? I promise to be very gentle . . . you won't regret doing it for the first time with me."

Strangely enough, she almost believed him for a minute. The warm whisper in her ear, the light fluttering of his lips on her cheek, and the tips of his fingers on her cleavage, so feather-like, made her wonder if she was just imagining the effect he had on her. The odor of his masculine sweat mixed with the smell of Neka 7 soap, the feel of his warm body pressing against hers, incinerating her to the core through her thin tricot shirt, were all so intoxicating. For a moment her world swirled and she lost her balance, lost herself in the uncontrollable urge to whisper back, "Yes, take me to your room. Bring me to your bed. Take me now, quickly, before I regain my self-control . . ."

She never knew whether those words had really passed her lips or remained as an echo in her head. Before she could find out, a thin female hand grabbed Tony by his belt and lifted him up in the air. Noa's energetic voice rang out loud and clear. "Come on cowboy. I'll let you ride me today 'cause I'm in the mood for playing and you play the game so well . . ."

Even years later, Mirale didn't know whether to thank Noa for her narrow escape from the clutches of unbridled debauchery or to hate her forever for snatching away that sweet promise of sensual intoxication. She hadn't been able to make up her mind about Noa ever since that time.

A few days after that conversation with Dina, the phone rang just as Mirale was getting ready to leave for the choir rehearsal for *Leil Haseder* (Passover Eve). It was Dina. "Mirale, do me a favor. I forgot the pages that I prepared for the people who read aloud from the *Hagada* (the traditional text read before Passover Eve dinner) at home. Can you go by my house and get them for me? They're on the dresser in my bedroom. I'm waiting for you in the dining hall. We're in the middle of rehearsals for *Leil Haseder*."

Mirale got on her bike and pedaled down the path leading to Dina and Yisrael's house. She hoped the house would be empty, because even though she had been given permission by the lady of the house to enter and retrieve the pages, she still felt a little uncomfortable trespassing. The door opened to an unfamiliar silence. She took a deep breath and went into the bedroom, trying not to look to either side. She picked up the pages from the dresser, but when she lifted them, an unexpected sight hit her eyes – a handsome naked man lying in a golden wheat field. Mirale blinked with embarrassment but it was too late. Her hand reached out, as if of its own accord, picked the book up, and put it into the plastic bag she was carrying.

Later, during the rehearsal, she imagined seeing shimmering light beaming from her innocent looking plastic bag and prayed no one else noticed the colorful rainbows glittering in the air around her. Contrary to her usual clear and meticulous articulation, she mispronounced words twice. After the rehearsal she apologized profusely and excused herself, explaining that she was tired from a long day at school, and went home as quickly as she could to hide the incriminating evidence that had by now burned a hole in her bag.

Only two days later, when she gets home earlier than usual, does she dare to take the book out of its hiding place. She closes the shutters and darkens the room, calculating the time she has for herself before the children come home at four o'clock. She has eighty minutes all to herself with no interruptions. She stretches out on her belly looking at the man in the wheat field on the cover of the book. He doesn't shy away from her penetrating look. His lips are slightly parted, his gaze confident and steady. The muscles on his belly are symmetrically curved, accentuated by the soft brown hair on his chest. The sun shines behind him, transforming the dry wheat stems into an illuminated golden foil that touches upon the curved outline of his broad shoulders. She reaches out with a hesitant hand, caresses his face, and opens the book.

What she sees inside makes her catch her breath. Although Dina had warned her that the photos were quite explicit, she hadn't mentioned that they were absolutely amazing. In spite of the total exposure of the male figures, there is nothing pornographic about them. The men are handsome, but not in an impossible, model-like way. They are as handsome like the cutest guys in class would be if they had just finished a round on the basketball court, all sweaty and virile. Their beauty is the attractive friendly type that holds no arrogance. Even the wild landscape where the photos were taken perfectly accommodates their rough, straightforward, warm manliness. All the men are handsome, but she takes a particular liking to the guy on the second page.

He has an honest and open face, trimmed with blond stubble, a military haircut, an innocent smile, soft, full lips (the kissing kind), a penetrating blue-eyed gaze, classic angled jaw, a wide hairy chest (but not too hairy), a piercing in the nipple (that's a novelty), and firm, brawny arms marked by prominent veins. His big hands are folded in his lap as he sits on the fender of his jeep in an oasis. He smile is aimed at Mirale and Mirale alone.

They met just a few days ago and the whole idea of a trip to the desert with someone who is, she has to admit, almost a stranger, is crazy but nonetheless enticing. The thought of letting him intimately touch her body is intimidating and she isn't sure she will be able to do it. However, at the same time there is also something very familiar about him, some elusive quality in his gaze, the way he talks, the music of his voice that makes her feel they have met before, a long time ago. This novel sensation of him being both strange and familiar dismantles her emotional barricades. She watches him, wondering why she doesn't feel at all embarrassed by his shameless nakedness. Without a second thought, she takes off her shirt. She is wearing only short pants and a bra. A content smile spreads slowly over his face and he quickly takes off his pants, leaving on his black underwear, and sits on the rug he has carefully laid on the grass. Leaning on his elbow, eyeing her thoroughly, the corners of his mouth twisting playfully, he pats the rug beside him, inviting her to sit next to him. "Aren't you going to join me?" he asks mischievously.

She hesitates for a moment, and then with a resolute expression, takes off her pants, exposing the expensive lace underwear, the pair she never believed she would have a proper occasion for wearing. His gives her a dazzling smile, showing two rows of perfectly white teeth. Before she can think about the next move, he has already taken off his underpants with one swift movement and is sitting on the rug again, one leg folded underneath him and one arm resting on the other, hiding the most interesting part of his anatomy. He examines her with an intense gaze that fills her with sudden warmth. The rush of heat travels from her pelvis all the way up to her neck and cheeks. She feels it flooding her cleavage and the soft curve of her breasts, which rise and fall with her quickening breath. Not taking her eyes off him, she puts her hands behind her back and unclasps her bra. When she takes it off, shaking her breasts free and feeling the light breeze caressing them, she hears him gasp and smiles.

Although her body is sweetly curved in a very feminine way, she has always thought of herself as chubby. She thinks her thighs are too thick, and her soft, round belly is a constant source of misery for her. But there's one part of her body she's proud of, the part that magnetizes men and brings up that adoring look that is so gratifying to see on their faces. Yes, her perfect breasts are the only part of her body that she really likes. In spite of their considerable size, they are round and firm, decorated by dark mocha-colored nipples that stare straight forward.

He rises slowly, and now it is her turn to gasp in admiration. His muscles dance as he moves in a very enticing way. She is enchanted by the gentle ripples that ebb and flow under his tanned skin. His body is so perfectly proportioned that watching him makes her ache with an uncontrollable yearning to touch him. He is brawny and strong. He has broad shoulders and a firm chest to lay her head against to listen to his heartbeat. Those beautiful sunken lines going down diagonally from his hips to his loins accentuate his narrow pelvis. He can't help noticing her open admiration and his smile widens. Her eyes are drawn to that place that was previously hidden by his thigh but now stands totally exposed before her. His organ moves as if it has a life of its own, brazen and shameless. It is lighter than the rest of the body, and colored a gentle blush color, like a ripe peach. It is surprisingly long, and it moves upward and to the side, as if watching her closely. The foreskin rolls back, decorating the head of his penis like a wreath. He takes his penis in his hand, caressing it from base to head with his long fingers, enjoying her appreciation.

"Do you like it?" he asks softly. She nods, feeling that speaking is a task beyond her power now, while she is hypnotized by his proximity. She inhales his scent, an odor of light masculine sweat and virile passion that sets her head spinning. She slides her hand down her belly, into her panties and the warm, hairy crevice, which is already moist with passion. She starts rubbing her finger up and down, very slowly, every now and then dipping it deeper inside. Her breath quickens as the rubbing becomes more vigorous. He steps towards her and puts his hands on her hips, slowly caressing her thighs as he kneels before her. He slides her panties down, gently kissing every piece of skin in his wake. She feels his kisses pulsating on her skin, sending tremors of warmth up her spine. After freeing her from her panties and tossing them aside, he gets up and hugs her.

"You are so beautiful to me," he whispers in her ear and his hot breath enhances the waves of heat that are travelling up and down her spine. "I feel my body melting into yours, melting where you touch me. I want to be one with you so very much. I crave to be inside you, to feel the bond between us, gentle and strong, soft and everlasting, until we don't feel the boundaries between us anymore, until we don't know where my body ends and your body begins."

His hot breath in her ear, the loving words he whispers to her, and the soft kisses he plants on her neck in between his whispers are all too powerful a combination to resist. She gives up all attempts at self-control. Her knees become jelly and she holds on to him, hanging on to his neck for dear life. He hugs her, holds her tight, not letting her fall. As she clings to him, her breasts squeezed against his hairy chest, she feels his rock hard erection pressing against her belly and the echoing answer of sweet throbbing in the circular muscles that clench rhythmically around her love tunnel.

"I want you, too," she whispers to the triangular indentation at the base of his neck. "Take me now, quickly, before I regain my self-control . . ."

"My sweet darling," he whispers, "I'm on the verge of explosion but I'm holding myself back. I don't want us to rush into it. I'd like to enjoy every second of this wonderful experience with you. I want to caress you slowly. Every inch of your body is erotic and I want to have it all, inch by inch. I promise to be gentle with you. We have all the time in the world." He bends his head to kiss her. Their lips touch and for a minute remain pressed together, not moving, as they get used to the taste and the smell of each other's breath. He smells like a fresh apple, crisp and juicy, and she longs to taste his tongue, but she waits for him, as he slowly moves his mouth over hers, sucking on her lower lip. Then he positions his mouth directly against hers and extends his tongue, which is soft and delicious. She meets his tongue with hers and they begin a slow dance of twisting and curling, every now and then retreating to swallow the sweet juices that fill their mouths. His hands are sliding up and down her back, feeling, squeezing, and then lightly fluttering. The almost imperceptible touch of his fingertips on her alert skin sends coded messages of pleasure that travel from the base of her spine to her head, making her swoon. She moans passionately, not finding the words to answer him, but hoping her moans will convey the sensual storm that is raging inside her.

Mirale turns and lies on her back. Her hand is wet with her own juices as her finger slides in and out of her love tunnel. Her thumb circles her clitoris, vibrating it rapidly. The quickened beating of her pulse drums in her ears, the room around her vanishes in a red haze, and the feeling of the approaching orgasm preoccupies all her senses.

Tony lowers her gently down on the cotton rug he has spread in the shade of the palm trees. The sun paints golden spots on her body, like the spots on a leopard's fur, and lights his body from behind so it looks radiant, surrounded by a halo of warm light. Deep and contemplative silence surrounds them, stretching as far as the blue mountains on the horizon. A light breeze murmurs in the leaves of the palm trees as if in wonder at the vapors of erotic excitement rising from these two naked bodies entwined in a loving embrace.

"Mummy, Mummy, where are you?" A cheerful voice shatters her daydream. Alarmed, Mirale shudders, pulls her hand out and wipes it on the sheet. The book falls to the floor with a heavy thud. She picks it up quickly and shoves it under the pile of books on her night dresser at the exact moment Tomer comes running into the bedroom.

"I found you Mummy!" He cheers. She smiles and sighs, "Indeed you have," hugging him tightly, apparently a little too tightly because he protests. "Mummy, you're suffocating me." She wipes a tear and lets him go.

On the way to supper in the Kibbutz dining-hall, Mirale and Eitan meet their good friends Dina and Yisrael. Immediately the men engage in a lively conversation about the situation in the factory, whether the economic difficulties experienced lately truly justify firing some of the workers, taking into consideration that they are loyal Kibbutz members who have been working there for ten or more years. Dina waits until they get a little further away and sneaks an inquisitive look at her friend. "Well?" she asks impatiently.

"Well, what?" Mirale replies innocently, trying to pretend she doesn't know what her friend is referring to.

"I know you took the book, so there's no point in denying it," Dina says, feeling perturbed.

"It's okay, really. You don't have to feel embarrassed. I was rather hoping you'd take it."

Embarrassed, Mirale only says, "Uh-huh," not daring to look her friend in the eye.

"Well? What's it like?" Apparently Dina isn't going to let her get away without answering.

"Nice," Mirale says in an uncommitted tone. "They invested a lot of effort in it, no doubt."

"That's it? Well-invested? That's all you can come up with? You didn't feel anything when you looked at the pictures of all those gorgeous men? Why don't we have such men on the Kibbutz? That's what I'd like to know." Dina rolls her eyes in mock disappointment. "Why we are forever doomed to look at Yossi's bulging belly, Amir's crooked legs, and . . .?"

"Okay, okay, I got the point." Mirale hastens to cut her friend short before she starts counting Eitan's physical shortcomings.

Dina smirks. "I bet looking at the pictures in that book gave you thrills you're not willing to admit, and I believe that tonight Eitan will be very grateful to me and to that book that I bought in Rome."

"Perhaps …" Mirale smiles mysteriously.

"Okay, go ahead and be cruel. Keep all the juicy details to yourself. Just remember who brought you the book and who told you everything that happened *after* she bought the book in Rome."

Hearing her friend's disappointed voice, Mirale hastens to promise her, "When I have something worth telling, you'll be the first to know."

While putting the children to sleep, Mirale is so distracted that she responds impatiently to their endless questions. When they ask for a story, she sings them a lullaby, and when they complain, she says with uncustomary firmness that today they will have to do with just a song. Her thoughts revolve around how to show Eitan the book and wondering how he will react to the pictures in it. Will he be agreeably excited as Yisrael was, or will he be horrified at the thought that she is so turned on by the explicit nudity? Maybe he will be angry with Dina for lending her the book (in an underhanded way) or with Yisrael for buying the book in the first place. Who knows how he might react? It might even spoil the friendship between the couples and that would be all her fault. Maybe she should just keep it a secret.

So Mirale keeps quiet about the book and doesn't tell Eitan anything, neither that evening nor in the evenings that follow. The week passes quickly. On Saturday Dina comes to visit her. While the children are playing outside together, she asks when Mirale is going to return the book to her. Mirale responds by saying she needs a little more time with it and that she will return it soon. Dina's curiosity is piqued.

"What exactly are you doing with my book?" She giggles. "Are you only spending time with it only during the early afternoon, or are you using it at night as well?"

Mirale blushes. "Oh my, how you've changed," she says a little bitterly. "You've started talking like Noa now."

"Is that so?" Dina is enflamed. "And pray tell me, your holy eminence, what does it mean to talk like Noa?"

"You know." Mirale shifts in her seat uncomfortably, trying to get over her friend's biting words. "Being open about all this . . . business, talking freely without thinking about who might overhear you and maybe later repeat what he has heard as a valuable piece of gossip during afternoon coffee in the neighborhood."

Dina considers this for a minute before answering. "You know what? You're right. I *have* changed, and I think it's for the *better* and I'm quite proud of it. Do you want to know something else? Yisrael is also pleased with the changes in me." Her voice becomes low and guttural. "Very, very pleased."

Mirale looks at her curiously. "Okay, I can see you owe me a few more stories . . ."

"Not before you tell me what you're doing with my book," protests Dina.

Mirale hesitates for a moment and then acquiesces. "All right, I'll tell you, but swear you won't tell anyone, not even Yisrael."

"Mirushka," Dina says in mock insult, "You know me. My lips are sealed." She moves her finger across her mouth to emphasize her vow of silence.

"Well, I," says Mirale, somewhat embarrassed, "I have been imagining I'm having an affair with one of the guys there."

"Really? Who is it?" Dina is clearly interested, accepting her friend's confession to having an imaginary love affair very naturally, to Mirale's great relief.

"How can I say which one? I don't know everybody's name, except for Tony, of course."

Dina narrows her eyes, and says nonchalantly, "Well, of course his name is Tony. After all, he's Italian. Where did you two meet? Please, tell me everything."

"We met in the hotel," Mirale responds quickly, excited at being able to share her great adventure with her best friend. "We both came alone, without our spouses. He has never asked me whether I'm married so I haven't asked him either, and frankly I don't care. I know it's just a holiday romance and it'll be over as soon as I go home to Eitan. We've seen each other a few times in the pool. I watched him while he was swimming front crawl and butterfly style. You should have seen him swimming! He has an amazing body, so lean and muscular. He flashes through the water like a yummy chocolate arrow. His shoulder muscles curve so wonderfully when he swims and it's just fascinating to watch him."

"Mm hmm," Dina nods in agreement, enjoying her friend's enthusiasm.

"I also swim a lot and so we started talking about how many laps we swam and how much colder the water was in the morning. Just small talk nonsense, you know, but I could feel his eyes burning as he was looking at me, burning me up from within."

"Yes," says Dina dreamily, "I know that look. Many years ago Yisrael looked at me like that, but not since then, not until we were in Rome, that is . . . Then he gave me that incinerating look again and God, how it turned me on! So what did you two do besides exchanging hot looks?"

"I don't know whether I want to share all these intimate details with you," Mirale teases her friend, but seeing Dina's frown she laughs and continues her story about the trip to the oasis, the light breeze caressing their naked bodies, and the sweet words he whispered in her ear, which turn her on more than anything else.

"So you haven't done anything yet except for making out?" Dina is slightly disappointed.

"No, but today is the big day," Mirale whispers to her. "Tonight I'm planning to go all the way and have intercourse with him!"

"Tonight?" Dina wonders.

That night Mirale lies with Tony for the first time. After a few enjoyable days of flirtation and courting in which he has provoked her body to the point of no return, she decides she is going to make the first move. She invites him to her room and Tony accepts her half-stammering invitation with a wide smile. "I'll be counting the minutes until we meet, my princess," he says, looking up at her after kissing her hand. She giggles uncontrollably, liking the chivalrous gesture.

She makes many preparations before the night falls. Candles are placed around the room, a thin ribbon of scented smoke rises in the air from the cedar and lavender incense stick, and the heavenly music of Terry Oldfield is playing in the background. Tony is a little surprised to see the romantic setting but it's evident from the expression on his face that he likes it a lot. She undresses him slowly, his skin glowing reddish-brown in the candlelight. He smiles at her excitedly, enjoying being handled in such an attentive manner. She takes her time undressing him, feeling his shoulder and chest muscles and all the way down his arms to his hands, which clutch her fingers longingly. She extends her tongue and touches one of his nipples. His breath catches. Satisfied with her success, she starts circling his nipple slowly with her flaxen tongue. When she reaches the tip of the nipple she nibbles it lightly. He lets out a deep groan and tilts his head back. She moves her attention to his other nipple, but continues to caress the one she has just left. He moans again and begs her to go further down. She complies, lingering on his belt and zipper, inserting her warm hand and cupping his awakening erection before taking his trousers off and fully exposing it. He gasps, his hands caressing her shiny auburn tresses.

She kneels before him and he steps out of his trousers. She gets up again, brushing her breasts against his legs, thighs and his hard erection as she rises to meet his eager lips. He kisses her softly at first, and then their tongues start dancing. His tongue is more demanding now, invading her mouth, filling it with a sweet fruity taste. He sucks on her tongue until she has to free her mouth to breathe a little. He plants one last wet kiss on her lips and delves between her breasts while his hands move slowly over her back, her bottom and her thighs, making her body tremble and her skin flush with goose bumps. He continues caressing her gently with the tips of his fingers and lightly scraping her skin with his nails as he goes down to the back of her knees and then between her legs, building tension around the focal point of her body, her moist crevice of hidden pleasures. His fingers comb the small, tight curls of pubic hair, every now and then sliding slowly into her simmering crack, which has started dripping. He bends to sniff the sweet scent of her awakening passion and tastes the honey drops on the tip of the crevice.

His hands caress her whole body with long motions, from head to toe, while his tongue explores her soft curves, marking long trails of sensual arousal, leaving no spot uncared for. His tongue sends shuddering wavelets of pleasure throughout her body that his caressing hands calm down. Oscillating between these opposites, she loses track of how long he toys with her in that manner, but suddenly she feels shock waves rising and going through her body. Her thighs close firmly on his hand, not letting it move until the waves subside. Then she pulls him to her, whispering in his ear, "Come to me, my love. Come to me now."

He eagerly sinks himself inside her, feeling her body's reaction as her pelvis rises to meet his with a thud that sends small electrical shocks up his spine. She looks into his beautiful brown eyes, which are brimming with love, and feels her whole body melting and opening up to him. He starts moving inside her while watching her face with great concentration. Her eyes are half-closed and her mouth opens slightly in a muffled cry as he increases the pace more and more. Captured in the intensity of the moment, she releases all attempts at control and lets herself go, getting carried away by the overpowering rhythm. He pounds into her with all his might and she holds him by the shoulders, amazed at his stamina. Another shock wave goes through her, erasing all awareness of the world outside her skin, but at the same time, she *is* the entire world outside of her skin.

When she regains consciousness, she sees his face twisting with that expression of acute pleasure that she loves to see on him. After a few more seconds he collapses on top of her with a deep sigh. She hugs him tight, tasting his sweat, inhaling his familiar scent, the same scent she has been breathing in for the past fifteen years. "I love you," she whispers. He kisses her neck and whispers in her ear, "I love you too, my wife."

Eitan

Eitan yawns widely and stretches his arms above his head. The constant drumming of the rain on the shutters brings a drowsy smile to his face. The sweet idleness of rainy days is but a small compensation for the exhausting days he spends in the fields throughout the year. The field workers, nicknamed *Falahim*, pride themselves on being the most hard-working members on the Kibbutz, sometimes working from sunrise to sunset in the burning hot season of the watermelons. They are always the last to arrive at the dining hall for dinner, with their muddy boots and dirty work clothes, demanding to be fed, enraging the kitchen workers who have just finished washing the floor. So in the rainy season they feel entitled to show up at the dining hall for a late breakfast in their most comfortable training pants, checked, zipped up sleepers and old army coats. Mirale has already gone to school and taken the children with her, so Eitan is free to sleep for as long as he pleases. He yawns again, relishing these lazy moments in bed, free from the pressing need to get up to work.

He rolls over onto his belly, leaning his head on his folded arms. A colorful cover from the pile of books on the night dresser on Mirale's side of the bed draws his attention. He pulls the big book out, thinking it must be a new cookbook. Maybe it contains more recipes for the rich chocolate cakes he likes, but when his eyes focus on the half-naked man smiling at him from the cover, he catches his breath. What *is* this book and what is it doing on Mirale's night dresser? Mirale, who never lets him put on a pornographic movie in the video player, has a book with pictures of naked men! She must have gotten it from someone. He knows she would rather die a thousand times than buy a book like this herself. Who could have given it to her? Maybe she is having an affair? No… He chases the thought out of his mind like waving off a nagging fly. No, it can't be. Not Mirale. It must have been Noa, that slut. She has been going after every man on the Kibbutz for years and she has finally run out of options so she must be fantasizing about foreign ones.

Burning with curiosity, Eitan opens the book and starts flipping through the pages. The photos are quite attractive, very professional, he decides. He inspects the models' male organs closely, trying to decide which of them are longer than 13.5 centimeters, and which are less. Some of the men are clearly non-Jewish, he thinks, but when their dicks are erect it's hard to tell because the foreskin folds under the head in a very sneaky way. A small image attracts his attention. It is unusual among all the photos of naked men in their full glory that are spread across one full page. This small photo portrays waves splashing against a rocky beach. There are two naked white men on the beach, one lying on his belly and the other bending over him. Eitan wrinkles his forehead trying to figure out exactly what is going on between the two of them, when he suddenly feels the familiar stretching and hardening movement in his loins. Horrified, he throws the book down as if it were a poisonous snake and gazes at his erect penis, which has raised its head expectantly, clearly eager and ready for action.

Oh no! Oh God, please no, it's not happening to me! No way, it's just some sort of a reflex, an automatic thing. There's certainly an erotic ambience here after last night, and it's morning, I always get a boner in the morning, but I never have time to do anything about it… Where are my *Playboy* magazines? I've told Mirale not to take them out of my drawer, but she always takes them and stuffs them God-knows-where when she gets the urge to tidy up the house. "What if Tomer should find it?" she asks me with that sanctimonious tone of hers. "He's in kindergarten!" I tell her, but she insists that as parents we have a responsibility to prevent the kids from seeing such material. Then she goes and leaves *this* hot stuff in her pile of books. Where are the goddamn magazines?

Enraged, Eitan pulls out the drawers of the night dresser and spills their contents onto the floor. He opens the wardrobe and pokes between the neatly folded clothes on the shelves. 'Mirale is going to kill me,' the fleeting thought crosses his mind, but right now the urgent need to find his *Playboys* drowns out all other thoughts. At last, at the bottom of the wardrobe, under a stack of well-folded, used plastic bags, he finds his magazines. With a sigh of relief he throws them on the bed and opens all of them at once, looking for the most explicit pictures. He spits on his hand and starts masturbating with rigorous, almost desperate movements until the moment of release. Breathing hard, he collapses on the magazines that are spread out on the bed.

I've got to get out of here. This happened because of rainy day idleness. Maybe I should go to the garage to visit Uri. He promised me the John Deere would be "fixed and ready yesterday," with his smug smile, not knowing we've all grown tired of his stale joke, especially since when it comes to him "yesterday" never seems to arrive. Hananya will probably offer me a cup of black coffee and some juicy tale about his latest sexual escapade. He always tells such tales of adventures about the days he runs errands as the Kibbutz's "house chauffeur." Hananya's tales leave the other men on the Kibbutz wondering what women find attractive in this scrawny Yemenite. Even after eliminating fifty percent of his tales as wild exaggerations, he still comes off as horny as a goat.

As "house chauffeur" of the Kibbutz, Hananya is responsible for running many errands. Anyone who needs to go to the doctor (who only comes to the Kibbutz once a week, but on other days can be visited on one of the other Kibbutzim or Moshavim in the area), or anyone who needs to buy something that cannot be found in the Kibbutz's small convenience store, calls Hananya. Since the Kibbutz is two hours away from Tiberias and a nearly four-hour drive from Tel-Aviv, it doesn't make sense to waste precious working days on things that the members need to buy in those places. So they tell Hananya what they need, whether it's a new bicycle or a double bed, and Hananya picks it up for them. Of course they're not always happy with his choices, especially since he's color blind, but then he recites his motto, 'you take what you get,' and nobody can think of a good answer to that. What most members don't know is that he decides where to buy things according to the proximity of his nearest "fuck-buddy." He even has this address book where women are arranged according to proximity... at least one in each of the surrounding towns and villages.

Eitan smirks at the memory of Hananya in his month of reserve duty. Everybody else was just doing their rounds – guarding, patrolling, and telling jokes, the kind horny reserve-duty soldiers tell when they haven't seen their wives for two weeks – but Hananya somehow managed to convince the battalion commander to grant him a special "after hours" permit because he couldn't concentrate unless he got laid at least once a day. Eitan remembers hearing Hannaya asking their commander for this special permit. He was certain the commander would scream at Hananya for such audacity but instead he just smiled and signed his "after hours" permit.

'O yes,' Eitan thinks, 'Hananya is the man I need to see right now to clear my head of all this stupid business. I need to forget it even happened.'

Late that night, when Mirale finally comes to bed, Eitan can't resist the urge to ask her who she got the book from, even though he had promised himself he would never ask. Embarrassed, Mirale tries to laugh it away, telling him she got it from Dina, who had brought it back from the weekend she and Yisrael spent in Rome.

She should really give it back she adds, as she's had it for quite some time now. She wants to ask him whether he has seen only the cover or whether he has also looked inside, but she doesn't dare. The mere thought of her husband looking at Tony's picture smiling at *her* from the desert oasis makes her cheeks burn. She is relieved when Eitan doesn't seem interested in pursuing the subject.

He lies with his eyes closed, praying she doesn't keep on talking about the book. To his great relief he hears her quiet breath after a few minutes, which tells him she is fast asleep. The memory he has refused to let his mind access for so many years, the memory that presses the panic button, bringing tears to his eyes, is about to rise. He feels it pressing against the wall of silence he has built around it. Careful not to wake Mirale he gets up, puts on his army coat and goes outside into the cool night air. The crescent moon is hanging low above the hemlock tree and the sky is full of stars. He drinks in the fresh air, letting it wash over his burning face. He's not in the mood to meet anyone. Thankfully the chances of that happening are slim at this time of night, so he heads to the circular road surrounding the Kibbutz for a walk. The chirping of crickets and his heavy breathing are the only sounds that disturb the calm nocturnal silence. The jackals have stopped howling and gone to sleep. When he walks past the cow shed he hears the lonely mooing of a cow separated from her calf.

Mirale must never know. He clenches his fists, fighting the unwanted moisture forming in his eyes. No one must ever know. The only one who knows his secret is Avishay, but he will never tell, he wouldn't dare. It was just adolescent mischief, he argues passionately with himself, why am I making such a big thing out of it? But deep down he knows it could be much more than that. Something lurks there that he has never allowed himself to explore, even though Avishay showed him the entrance on that stormy evening, many years ago when Raz was sick and went to sleep at his parents' apartment, so Eitan and Avishay were alone together in the children's house.

It was an exceptionally cold and stormy winter night and neither the night guard nor the night nanny would go outside into the storm for anything other than the shrill cries of screaming babies. The wind was raging outside, howling through the shutters like a pack of wolves. Lightning illuminated the room in ghastly white flashes and thunder exploded above. Avishay asked him if he could sleep in his bed and Eitan moved aside, making room for him in the narrow bed. Avishay's warm body squeezed against his side. His feet were cold and his breath was warm against Eitan's neck. Eitan lay on his back, trying to ignore the strange sensations that surged through his body, when suddenly he felt a movement in his penis. He almost stopped breathing, fearing Avishay would notice what had happened to him. He couldn't even roll over to his side to hide his rising erection.

To his great surprise, Avishay extended his arm and gently touched the tent that was created in his pajamas. Eitan's reaction to the warm touch was beyond his ability to control and against his will he heard himself groan. Without a word Avishay unbuttoned the fly, set his erect organ free and dove under the blanket. After a minute Eitan felt the soft touch of Avishay's lips and a warm wet tongue on the sensitive skin of his taut organ. His hands twisted, clutching the sheet. He felt his whole being compress into that hot spot, completely absorbed in the touch that sent quivering waves of excitement higher and higher until he couldn't hold it in anymore and felt the warm fluid shooting out of him. After a long moment of silence he said with a harsh voice, "The day you tell anyone what happened here will be your last. I'll do you in. Do you understand? Now go back to your bed." Avishay pursed his lips in bruised silence and got out of Eitan's bed. In a sharp flash of white lightning, Eitan thought he saw the wet trail of a tear running down Avishay's cheek, but he hardened his heart and didn't say a word.

Years later, when one of the guys mentioned he had heard a rumor that Avishay had come out of the closet, the guys weren't surprised by the news. "Avishay has always been a gentle boy with a suspicious inclination for art," Eitan remarked scornfully. "I've always suspected that little shit was a cocksucker, judging by the way he used to wiggle his ass from side to side while walking and the way he used to eye me in the common shower."

In the days and weeks that followed the field workers noticed strange changes in Eitan's behavior. The usually energetic man who scolded them for every moment of idleness was seen staring blankly into the air while holding the ring he was supposed to screw onto a pipe. When they asked him, "What is it?" he stirred, and with a strange look on his face started messing with the pipe as if trying to hide his embarrassment. When some of the young workers, fresh from the army, took off their shirts and started a water fight on a particularly hot morning after breakfast, Eitan reprimanded them sharply. He worked for ten hours a day with unrelenting determination and would stay in the field even longer if it weren't for his friends' open resentment. In the evenings he was so tired that he barely made it to the end of the News at eight, and usually fell asleep on Tomer's bed in the middle of reading him a bedtime story.

At first Mirale accepted the long work hours with understanding, but when weeks turned into months and there was still no sign of change, she openly expressed her growing annoyance. Now she has run out of patience when Eitan tells her on a Saturday morning that he won't be able to go for a hike to their favorite view point with her and the kids because he has to open the irrigation in the fields. They are still in bed so she raises herself onto her elbows and snaps at him in her strictest voice, "No! You're not going, not on a Saturday morning. That's outrageous!"

Surprised by her unfamiliar determination, Eitan asks, "Why? Is there something special going on this Saturday?"

"In fact there is. I'm here and you're here. The kids are still asleep and it's the first time in months that I've seen you awake and able to talk to me, instead snoring on the sofa in front of the TV. So forget the irrigation. You're going nowhere, Mister!"

A content smile spreads across Eitan's face. The firm demand in that unfamiliar authoritative voice is pleasing, very pleasing. "So… what are you going to do about it?" he teases her in amused defiance.

She picks up on his amused, interested tone and pretends to weigh her options seriously. "Ahammm, I have to think about it… clearly you deserve to be punished for the last few months."

"You're right," he readily agrees. "I've really neglected

you and the kids. So how do you intend to punish me for that?"

"*Maybe…*" she prolongs that last syllable with a tone of conspiracy, "maybe I'll tie you to the bed with your legs spread apart, on your back…"

"No," he stops her short, "not on my back, on my belly."

Mirale looks at him, surprised, but goes along with his whim. "Okay, so you'll lie on your belly and I'll tie you to the bed posts and start punishing you severely."

These last words evoke an immediate response from his eager penis, but at that moment Tomer jumps onto their bed and Eitan rolls onto his side, embarrassed. Mirale sighs, hugs Tomer and whispers in Eitan's ear, "Never mind darling, to be continued in the evening."

So it happens that on that particular Saturday Eitan doesn't go to open the irrigation in the fields. Instead he plays with his children and helps Mirale make lunch while their short conversation from the morning constantly plays back in his mind. He doesn't know what made him tell her to tie him on his belly. He has never thought of asking her to do it before, but now that he has asked, and has felt the direct influence of this request on his expectant penis, he is eager to consummate the scene that sends such thrilled shudders down his spine, just from thinking about it.

That evening they put the children to bed early, tell Yossi they are exhausted and therefore cannot come to the Kibbutz members' weekly assembly, lock the door, close the shutters, make sure the children are asleep and stand in their bedroom looking at each other with shy expectation.

Mirale takes the initiative. "Would you like me to fulfill your fantasy?" she asks him softly.

Eitan hugs her close, absorbing the familiar warmth of her body. The words are on the tip of his tongue but refuse to come out explicitly. "I..." he whispers in her ear, "I'd like you to..."

Mirale understands his difficulty expressing something very different from their usual lovemaking. "Would you like me to tie you on your belly?"

He nods, tightening his hug until she can hardly breathe. "And what else would you like me to do to you?"

He doesn't say anything so she tries to use her imagination. "Would you like me to stroke you all over your body with my hair?"

He confirms with a nod. "Would you like me to lick you from top to bottom?" He nods vigorously.

Encouraged by her successful guesses, she next asks with a soft whisper, right into his ear, "Would you like me to put a finger up your ass?"

His body goes rigid. His lips become a thin line as he feels a hot convergence in the center of his body. He is seized by a turbulence of conflicting emotions. Is this really what he wants? What he has always secretly craved? Is this what freaked him out? To find this out about himself? What does it say about him? Does it mean he's gay? And if he's really gay, Mirale mustn't know. It would kill her to know that.

Mirale doesn't understand fully but she senses some inner conflict has made him freeze. She strokes his hair and whispers, "I read it in a guide book for better sex, in the chapter titled 'How to Please Your Man.' It says that if you insert a finger into your man's ass while stroking his organ, his pleasure is doubled. It has something to do with the prostate gland. The book really recommends it. Would you like to try that, my sweet?"

Eitan's body loosens up at the words 'guide book.' If it's written there it must be something that a lot of men do, not just gay men. Maybe he can try it, and it won't necessarily mean he's gay. "Yes," he whispers with bashful enthusiasm, "I'd like to."

Mirale undresses him slowly, taking her time to kiss every exposed area of skin. Eitan closes his eyes, relishing the flitting touch of her lips on his naked body. She lays him on the bed and ties his hands to the bedposts with colorful silk scarves. Then she puts a little pillow under his belly and spreads his legs apart. He feels her long soft hair slowly dragging over his bare skin, from head to toe, swirling and caressing, like a thousand tiny silk fingers. He can't tell whether it is tickling, spine-tingling or tormenting in the most wonderful way. All he knows is that his whole body has been transformed into a giant receiver of physical sensations and his skin detects even the tiniest of them in great anticipation of what is yet to come.

When her hair touches his buttocks he raises them a little, just a tiny movement, but she notices it. She starts licking and kissing the nape of his back and works her way down along his spine to that secret, tightly clenched crack between the cheeks of his ass. She strokes it lightly, passing her fingers up and down the crack until it loosens up a little and lets her explore deeper. She spreads the cheeks and starts licking the hairy pathway that leads all the way down to the pink flower that is still in the bud. With her other hand she reaches under him to stroke his soft balls and his erect organ, which is already very taut.

For a moment he freaks out. Where the hell did she pick up all these moves? She has never done this to him before, that's for sure. Maybe another man has asked her to do it for him? He quickly chases the ugly thought away by repeating the mantra "guidebook" over and over again until he feels calm enough to relax back into the rhythm of the exciting new sensations that rise in his body at the touch of her hands on this area he has never paid much conscious attention to before.

When she notices she is unable to reach his penis and grab it tightly, as he likes her to, she turns him onto his side and flexes his upper leg. He obeys her willingly, relishing that obedient pose that has turned him into a submissive novice, a vessel for receiving pleasure. She lies beside him with her head on his thigh. Now she can conveniently reach his testicles, which shrink a little under her tongue, as well as that smooth, pink wreath around his anus. She extends her tongue, hesitantly at first, touching it with only the pointed tip of her tongue, but then, amazed by her own audacity, she starts licking it in smaller and smaller concentric circles until her tongue touches the very center of the vortex, and even goes in a little. She hears him gasp and moan. "Do you like it like this?" She asks bashfully.

"Yeah," he says gasping, "don't stop." She goes on licking, her tongue delving deeper and deeper into the tight hole, which slowly opens up to her. Her other hand continues rubbing his throbbing organ until he feels he won't be able to last much longer. Tidal waves of quivering sensations, almost too powerful to resist, sweep over him, but he wants to prolong it for just a while longer. Summoning his courage, he whispers, "Stick your finger in, now." She spits into his pinkish well and gently starts drilling it with her finger, deepening her thrusts, millimeter by millimeter. Eitan hears someone groaning long guttural groans that echo and deepen and become louder and louder as Mirale deepens her drilling into his virginal anus. He feels the waves closing over his head as he clutches the sheet and the hot semen pools and shoots out of him with a liberating roar.

For a while he lies there, folded on his side, trying to catch his breath and make sense of what has just happened. Mirale hugs him from behind, wondering what his reaction will be. Will he want to do it again, or will he be ashamed of the freedom he has allowed her to take with his body? She has certainly just done some things she never imagined herself doing. But now that she has, and has seen the effect it had on him, she rather likes it. She yearns for him to ask her whether she wants similar treatment as his intense groans, clearly demonstrating how profound his pleasure has been, have excited her immeasurably. Eitan is also wondering what to say at this point. Her open readiness to give him pleasure in an unconventional way pleases him, but at the same time it's also a cause for worry. He never thought she was capable of doing such things.

When they first started having sex and he had wanted to lick her *down there* she had refused to let him do it. It took him a long time to convince her that it wasn't dirty, that the taste was really good and that there was nothing immoral or debasing about it. He had to reassure her that he took pleasure in it as well as her before she would let him eat her up.

Now… from a sex kitten she has transformed into a sex tiger! For a moment he isn't sure whether he approves of the change, but then the memories of the last few moments reverberate through his body, convincing him that it's all for the best. He feels she expects some sort of reciprocation from him. Turning to her, he kisses her cheeks, her eyes and her forehead. Embracing her closely, he whispers one word in her ear that puts a loving smile on her face.

Esther

Esther's naturally bouncing curls become her little round face and her smile is always ready at the corners of her mouth, just waiting for the smallest reason to light up her face, sometimes for no reason at all. She has a generous, blazing, all-white-teeth smile that is adorned by two dimples on her cheeks. Her cynical remarks would probably be met with a much stronger reaction if they weren't accompanied by that melting smile. If you want to find Esther, all you have to do is look around for a group of laughing people and she will surely be in their midst. The kitchen workers swore they could no longer withstand the difficulty of their work after Esther was transferred to the Kindergarten. The dining hall workers, who were usually temporary workers, like Gar'in members before being drafted to the army, or mothers fresh from maternity leave, started flooding the work committee with complaints about their supervisor's demeaning attitude now that Esther was no longer in charge.

The jovial conduct that makes everyone like Esther so much also makes her seem open and care-free. However, anyone who tries to probe deeper is met with a wall of fortified bashfulness. Even Yoram, her husband of fourteen years and the father of her children, has failed to bring that wall down, despite all his efforts, so he too has almost given up. She never makes love to him if there is any glimpse of light visible in the room. She makes him get up, put out every light in the house, including the small night light near the toilet, before she lets him touch her. He has tried to cajole her to undress before him, saying that the sight of her chocolate colored naked body arouses him, but to no avail. His pleadings to have a chance to actually see what he's doing to her *down there*, and not only feel it, so that he'll know how to please her better, are met with obstinate refusal. After a few years of futile attempts to get her to change her mind, he has resigned himself to respecting her wish for making love in the missionary position in total darkness. He no longer bothers mentioning the possibility of varying their customary routine with other sexual positions he has heard about through rumors, because he knows she will never agree.

Their lovemaking is agreed upon through a silent exchange of looks. Wild scenes of unbridled passion, the ripping off of clothes and the sweeping of tables that Hollywood movies are so fond of portraying, are stored on the science fiction shelves as far as Esther and Yoram are concerned. Sex is a highly regulated ritual in which both parties have an agreed upon set of motions that have been well practiced. This serves to decrease the tension and create a nice, comfortable atmosphere that allows for reasonable satisfaction. On the rare occasions when Yoram tries to change something in the order of things, Esther makes it very clear that she is perfectly happy with the way things are and sees nothing that merits change, not even one detail of their private ceremony.

Late at night Esther sits down in her favorite armchair, warming her hands on a last cup of tea before bedtime, relishing the silence around her, which is disturbed only by the sound of the calm breathing of her sleeping children and the light snoring of Yoram. He has gone to bed much earlier but she feels the need for these quiet moments of silence in the deep of the night. She sets the alarm clock for six o'clock and calculates quickly that she has five and a half hours left to sleep, if Uriel doesn't wake up. She prays silently, to whichever deity is listening at the moment. 'I pray he doesn't wake up. Is this too much to ask of you, God? That you make one small child sleep until the morning?'

Her prayer is answered, and the next thing she is aware of is the annoying sound of the alarm clock. She jumps out of bed and runs to check on Uriel. Only after making sure that his chest is rising and falling regularly, she lets out a sigh. A wide smile spreads across her face. Five and a half hours of uninterrupted sleep, no nightmares, changing wet sheets and having to make hot cocoa in the middle of the night! She can't remember when last she had such a treat. Esther's wider than usual smile attracts Noa's attention when Esther enters the convenience store on the Kibbutz to get some things for the Kindergarten.

"How was this night different from all other nights?" Noa asks with her familiar witty sarcasm, paraphrasing the famous first line of the Four Questions of Passover. She is passing products with agile movements, while glancing at Esther. Not even bothering to lower her voice when she asks brusquely, "Did you get laid?"

Esther feels the reddish hue in her cheeks beginning to spread to her forehead and neck. She resents her tendency for child-like blushing and resents Noa for making her blush. "Noa, enough," she says with dismay, "you know how I hate it when you start talking funny."

The mild reproach only pours gas on Noa's burning curiosity. "First admit that I am right," she chuckles, "and besides, when have you ever heard anyone over five years old say 'talk funny?' No doubt working in the Kindergarten is affecting you, and for the worse."

"If you really want to know," Esther says defiantly, "my good mood comes from the fact that Uriel didn't wake up in the night and I was granted a full night's sleep for a change."

"Okay, okay," Noa tries to appease her, "whatever you say. Listen, I've got something huge to tell you. In two weeks' time we're going on a jeep tour! No-o," she waves a warning finger in front of Esther's disbelieving eyes. "I've already talked to Batya, Dina, Shulinka and Mirale, and they're all so excited. Who wouldn't be? Listen to this: a three-day tour in jeeps, just us girls, happy and care-free, no children, no husbands, no cooking, and no work! Just going out into the wild, bonding with mother earth, sleeping outside around a campfire, having the time of our lives! What do you say?"

Esther smiles dreamily. "It sounds wonderful, but…"

"No buts!" Noa interrupts her sharply. "I already told you that I've made up my mind and we're going. You just have to let the human resources manager that he has to find you a replacement in the Kindergarten for those dates. Yossi will probably freak out and start yelling at us… how can we do this to him, giving him notice only at the last minute, and if we think he's going to pull out workers from the manufacturing sections like the plastic factory, or the Falha (field workers), we can forget about it… but you know what? I don't give a flying fuck! All his screaming and yelling doesn't even make a dent in my nipple!"

In spite of her apprehension, Esther bursts into a bell-like peal of laughter. There are a few things she doesn't like about Noa, especially her straightforward attitude regarding all things that should be done and kept in the dark, but there's one quality Noa possesses that she's unsurpassed in, and that's getting things done. She's a doer, a go-getter, no doubt about that. When she sets her mind to doing something, come hell or high water, you can be sure she'll get it done in the end. However, there are some moments during the next few weeks that made it seem like Noa's determination and the girls' obvious enthusiasm about their all-girl getaway are not enough to make it happen.

The obstacles are varied and numerous. They have to find someone to help Chocho, Shulinka's husband, who insists he can't take care of teenage children for three whole days. They put their foot down in the argument with Yossi, the human resourses manager who claims he can't let Batya miss Apple class on a Friday when all the children are at home, because the parents would surely have some very nasty things to say to him afterwards. The general secretary of the Kibbutz complains at the members' weekly assembly that it is unthinkable that the convenience store will be closed for 3 whole days, and the factory workers are enraged at being enlisted to fill in for the missing nannies in the children's houses. Lastly they have to convince Dina, who gets cold feet at the last minute, that her children will not suffer permanent and irreversible mental damage if she is absent for three days.

Esther watches Noa admiringly as she wages battle against all the forces of evil that conspire to cancel their trip – spoiled husbands, heartless human resources managers, worried parents, enraged factory workers and maternal guilt. Noa convinces, reproaches, cajoles, orders, pleads, improvises, plans, calls and proclaims; and finally announces that on Thursday, at six in the morning, everyone should be present with all their equipment in the parking lot, ready to move out. And so it happens, and so they set off on their trip.

They're elated, not letting anything bring them down, not the bumps in the dusty dirt roads or the two chauvinistic drivers who have already started licking their lips as they think about spending the night with a bunch of care-free, husband-free women. Dinner around a camp fire by Lake Kinneret (Sea of Galilee) is twice as tasty since the two drivers make it while the girls watch them tell jokes at their expense. When Batya wants to help them, Noa sits her down firmly. "Come on, Batya, you're on holiday now. Besides, we paid them a lot for their services so let them earn their money." The sun has already set behind the mountains of Galilee and the twinkling lights of Tiberias can be seen on the other side of the pool of darkness. The familiar smell of the Kinneret, the odor of reeds and sweet water, envelops them. They lie on mattresses around the fire, listening to the splashing of the wavelets on the smooth, round pebbles of the beach, passing a bottle of Yarden Emerald Riesling that slides smoothly down the throat. They feel inebriated with the night, as they enjoy these rare moments of freedom from their routine chores.

When the bottle is empty Noa suggests playing "Truth or Dare," and they accept her suggestion willingly. Most of the girls choose "Truth," and naturally most of the questions target the one issue that everyone is passionate about. The conversation around the fire becomes more and more heated, but not because of the flames that illuminate the women's faces. They are conspirators in a secret feminine circle that has left the rest of the world in the darkness behind them. Esther's amazement grows by the minute. A lot of the words being used are unknown to her, but after trying once or twice to get clarifications and receiving showers of laughter in return, she doesn't dare ask any more questions. She satisfies herself with listening attentively.

"Sixty-nine" sounds like a code name for some complicated military operation, and from what Batya tells them, she understands that it does require some degree of coordination. But she doesn't understand why, in Batya's story, Oren shouts when Batya bites him lightly after getting carried away by her own pleasure. Light biting feels nice in the moment of orgasm; Yoram does this to her shoulder when he comes. She also wonders about Michaela, who works with her in the Kindergarten, when she tells them that she likes "golden showers." Is the shower in her room at the Kibbutz not good enough for her? Why does she want a shower made of gold? Who does she think she is? An Arab sheikh? Esther is sure that all the girls share her disdain for Michaela's materialism because they stare at her, gaping, until Noa saves the day by spinning the bottle again.

The bottle spins around and comes to a halt, pointing at Dina. She opts for "Truth" first, but when she hears Noa's demand to give them a detailed account of everything she and Yisrael did in Rome *after* buying that famous book of hers, she changes her mind and goes with "Dare." But Dina should have known Noa wouldn't let her off the hook so easily. Like a Rottweiler, once she locks her jaws on something you can't take it away from her.

"I dare you to bring out the book and show us the hottest guy in it."

"Do you think I packed the book together with my tent and sleeping bag?" Dina snaps at her.

"Okay," Noa concedes. "So just describe him to us. I guess by now you've accumulated enough mileage on it in order to remember all of them."

"What book?" Esther asks surprised.

Noa gives her an incredulous look and chuckles. "Don't tell me you haven't heard about the book Dina brought back from Rome!"

"No, I really haven't. I'm sorry Dina," Esther apologizes. "I was busy and didn't have time to talk to you after you got back from Rome. What is this book? Is it an art book?"

"Ah-ha…" Noa prolongs the sound, "the art of the perfect male body!"

Mirale sighs in agreement and Noa immediately zooms in on her. "Who were you thinking about just now? Tell me," she tickles Mirale, "come on, spill it out…"

"Okay, okay," Mirale acquiesces, half choked with laughter. "I admit it, I've been thinking about the guy who is sitting in the desert on the fender of his jeep, the guy with the blond hair and the hypnotizing smile."

"Really? And what *other* hypnotic body part does he have?" Noa asks in a salacious tone.

"The important part," Mirale says.

Realizing she won't be able to get anything else from Mirale, Noa spins the bottle again and this time it points to Shulinka, who, to Noa's delight, chooses "Truth." Shulinka is a voluptuous woman, all soft curves with a beautiful pair of impressive breasts, the kind that leave men breathless and prompts Bedouin shepherds to offer a thousand camels for the right to marry the woman with the breasts.

Of all the things that Chocho does to you during your foreplay, what do you like the most?" Noa asks her with bright eyes.

Shulinka closes her eyes for a minute and unintentionally her hands drift almost imperceptibly towards her cleavage, caressing the soft skin of her breasts. "I like it when he kisses me from top to bottom and moves his lips ever so slowly along my neck and my breasts. The hair of his beard tickles me and gives me goose bumps all over. Then he goes south, further and further, and I feel my vagina clenching in anticipation. Finally, after torturing me with kisses behind my knees and along my inner thighs, which makes my knees turn to jelly, he spreads my legs and starts licking me slowly with his wide, soft, wet, warm tongue. He licks me from top to bottom and back again, up and down my vagina…"

Shulinka's voice is husky, almost guttural, and Esther feels gentle currents flowing, causing her to tingle *down there*. Irritated, she rubs the general area of her pubic rise through the thin cotton of her harem pants. To her surprise she discovers that the thin fabric is moist.

"Then, after licking me thoroughly, he makes his tongue pointy and starts poking it inside me, like he's fucking me with his tongue…"

At any other time in her life Esther would have been appalled by the explicit, colorful language Shulinka is using, but right now she finds herself out of breath, and to her surprise she feels a troubling humming in her private parts that is increasing by the second. She rubs it harder, trying to satiate that irritating itch, but her need just keeps growing and she feels she has to, simply must, insert a finger and rub herself a little from inside.

Shulinka continues talking in that dreamy, husky voice, her eyes half closed. "So he spreads my lips with his fingers and starts sucking on my clitoris, licking and sucking alternately. Then he does a little nibbling, very gently, with the tips of his teeth, but it's enough to make me catch my breath and send me reeling…"

The undertone of sighs around the campfire becomes stronger and stronger, rising and falling like the rustling of the wind in the leaves of the Eucalyptus tree under which they have set up their camp. Esther's finger accelerates the pace of the rubbing, as if of its own accord, and Esther's breathing catches.

"Then, when I start floating, he inserts two fingers

into my vagina and starts twisting them, drilling into my vagina, while continuing to lick and suck and nibble until I just freak out, losing my mind, losing myself…"

Esther bends over a little to hide the excited rubbing that has now turned into an insertion of two fingers, deeper and deeper, in and out, while her thumb keeps pressure on her clitoris. She is thankful the other women don't notice what she's doing to herself. They too are all breathing heavily now, their eyes on Shulinka, who doesn't seem to notice their presence, but goes on talking in her absorbed drone.

"I feel my knees turn to jelly. I start convulsing uncontrollably and seconds before I come he slams himself inside me, hard, again and again, and I scream so much that all our neighbors surely know that we're fucking, but I don't give a damn because I'm not myself… At that moment I'm nothing but a quivering lump of exposed nerves being fucked senseless, feeling sweet electrical shocks in my vagina, again, and again…"

Shulinka's voice trails off into a deep, longing sigh, echoing the choir of groans and moaning sighs around the campfire, which swallow up Esther's ecstatic sighs as well. Shulinka's story has brought the compressed sexual energy that pulsates throughout the throng of women to a climax, which is followed by a weird silence that cannot be dispelled despite Noa's persistent attempts to revive the conversation. Finally she gives up and the women disperse, each to her own sleeping bag, except for Esther who remains by the fire, gazing into the flames, trying to figure out what the hell just happened to her. She has never felt herself burning *down there* with such insatiable desire. Nothing could have stopped her probing fingers, or neither her natural bashfulness, the crowd around her, nor the presence of the two drivers in the distance. She desperately hopes that even if the other girls noticed what she was doing during Shulinka's engaging tale, they won't say anything to her about it tomorrow, or she'll just die of shame.

The next morning the early sun touches on Esther's eyelids, welcoming her to a crisp new day. Most of the women are still asleep. Only Batya is sitting by the campfire, stirring two little pots that are standing on the red coals. Esther joins her, deeply inhaling the smell of coffee slowly brewing on the fire mixed with the minty smell of the Eucalyptus leaves that Batya has spread on the coals.

"Did you sleep well?" Batya asks in a motherly tone.

"Yes," Esther yawns, even though she had been turning over in her sleeping bag all night, "fantastic."

"At last one quiet night, ha? Without having to wake up for anyone, right?" Batya smiles a sympathetic smile. "Don't worry, they grow up in the end and this phase passes somehow. Would you like herb tea or black coffee?"

"Coffee for me." Esther yawns yet another jaw-dislocating yawn.

Batya hands her a small cup of fresh coffee mixed with cardamom that smells divine, and sits down beside her. Esther warms her hands on the steaming mug, gazing into the flames.

"It was quite a night yesterday, wasn't it?" Batya whispers to her with a conspiratorial smile.

Still feeling guilty about her unusual experience, Esther wakes up from her reveries with a jolt and looks at Batya inquisitively, wondering where exactly she is going with that remark. Had she been seen? Had she been heard? But Batya carries on chatting merrily without betraying any sign of being aware of Esther's plight.

"This is how it always is when we are alone, just us girls. We are free, laughing carelessly… the energy in the group has an entirely different quality when there are no boys around. It's difficult to explain it…" Batya's voice trails off and she looks at Esther as if asking her to corroborate what she has just said. Esther shrugs, hoping that Batya doesn't pursue this particular topic of conversation. She is saved by Dina who comes to sit beside them. She is dressed in tight jeans and a tricot shirt, her face fresh and her hair combed high and caught in a ponytail, looking as beautiful as ever. Mirale, on the other hand, comes to the fire with a drowsy look on her swollen face, with a 'don't even think about talking to me before I drink at least two cups of coffee' yawn.

"It was pretty amazing, last night, wasn't it?" Batya tries her luck again with a new audience. This time she gets the response she is hoping for.

"Oh sure," Dina swings her pony tail energetically, "it was wonderful."

"Ah-ha," Mirale corroborates, "wonderful."

Encouraged by her supportive audience, Batya carries on. "Have you noticed the interesting fact that we behave differently when there are no men around? I'm sure that if we had had men with us last night, we wouldn't have been able to reach the level of openness and fun-filled horniness we experienced last night."

Mirale coughs with embarrassment, attributing it to the steaming coffee, but Dina gives Batya a wide smile of understanding.

"I'd like to tell you something," Batya whispers to Dina, giggling. "I got so horny last night like I haven't felt for a long time, with all this… talk around the fire."

"Really?" Dina asks sympathetically. "It's not like that with Menashe?" Batya shrugs and shakes her head no. After a moment of heavy silence she adds, "Maybe it was never like that with Menashe."

Dina doesn't have time to respond because one by one the women come out of their sleeping bags and tents, drowsy and yawning, their movements slowed down by the idleness of a free day, until Noa comes along, as energetic and talkative as ever.

"The Kinneret is as smooth as a mirror and the water isn't cold at all! Who's coming for a morning swim with me?"

Her question is left unanswered, hanging in the air. Batya, feeling her disappointment, says, "Wait a while, let them recuperate. You know what? Another cup of tea and I'm coming with you."

Noa thanks her with an acknowledging nod and sits by the glowing coals. As it turns out, Batya is right. After a few rounds of tea, coffee and some home-made cookies, everyone is much friendlier and more jovial, open to revolutionary suggestions like morning skinny dipping.

"Skinny dipping?" Esther is alarmed. "But won't people see us?"

"Who's going to come to this remote beach at this time of the morning?" Noa disregards her concern. "Don't worry, it's only us and the coots."

"But what about the drivers?" Esther's mind isn't at rest yet.

Noa smiles her sweet conspirator's smile. "I sent them to Tzemach mall to buy us fresh pita bread and all sorts of things for breakfast. It'll take them at least an hour to get back."

The women's eyes light up. "Come on, what are we waiting for?" Shulinka cries enthusiastically.

They stand on the water's edge. With the calm, green lake water lapping at their feet. They shriek at the touch of the cool water on their warm skin. They gets goose bumps as they make their way into deeper water. Their nipples harden and become pointy little antennas, broadcasting their delight at being so carefree. They laugh, scream merrily and splash around as they chase each other, making waves in the calm water. Of all the women, only Esther shows up with a bathing suit. Noa and Shulinka notice it and exchange a knowing smile, but don't say anything to her.

The women frolic in the dark green water, romping like kids on the first day of the summer holiday. Esther looks at her playful friends. Their wet skin is glowing in the golden rays of the morning sun and their breasts are bouncing up and down, confirming the necessity of this temporary release from the prison of their brassieres. They are a rejoicing pack of nymphs, celebrating this intense moment with all its colors, smells, and sensations, with the sun, the water, and the air that surrounds them and the land under their feet.

Suddenly Esther's expression changes and becomes resolute. She stands up in the shallow water, unfastens her bikini bra, takes it off and starts waving it, screaming triumphantly. For a moment they stare at her, amazed, then smile and join her with encouraging cries that turn to screams of encouragement, when after another minute Esther dives momentarily and then emerges waving the bottom part of her bikini as if it were a victory flag.

The water on Esther's skin feels somehow different now that every bit of her body is exposed to its gentle, cool caress. It allows her to absorb all of the sensory transmissions from her enhanced senses, highlighting the fact that this isn't just any ordinary day. The sun has risen, painting golden streaks on the calm water and filling Esther's heart with serene beauty. She breathes in the fresh aromas of the bitter-sweet reeds and Eucalyptus leaves. She joins her friends who are still prancing in the shallow water, supporting each other, hugging a wet waist, their breasts bouncing as they turn and turn in a bacchanalia of primal bliss and unbridled joy, the awakening of the body to sensual exultation.

Noa

Dina entered the convenience store, glanced around and sighed heavily. The hour after lunch on Fridays was always the busiest time of the week, the time when everybody was trying to get everything done before Shabbat. Almost all the Kibbutz members showed up at the convenience store then, and they all wanted Noa to finalize their bills as quickly as possible because they had to collect their clean laundry from the Laundromat and get to the children's home on time. Otherwise the nannies would get angry and start complaining that nobody thought about them. The nannies also had shopping to do for Shabbat, laundry to collect and their own children to pick up.

In the middle of all the turmoil, Noa was scanning prices diligently and writing down the charges on the members' cards. Her long, beautifully manicured fingernails, so outstanding in contrast to the nails of most of the Kibbutz women, were punching the numbers on the keyboard so quickly, they sounded like rap music. Dina noticed that today Noa was in a cheerful mood and each nail was painted a different color: purple, blue, green, yellow and orange… the colors of the rainbow, thought Dina. Only red was missing. Then she noticed Noa's toenails under the counter and she wasn't surprised to see that they were painted bright red. Dina exhaled a sigh of relief. At least one good thing would come out of this crowded hour in the convenience store. Noa wouldn't be able to grab hold of her like she had the day before, when she caught her on the path on her way home and started interrogating her about the book she brought back from Rome, which is all the girls were talking about when they met for afternoon coffee on the neighborhood's public lawn.

What ticked Noa off was the fact that for some mysterious reason, Dina had shown the book to everyone, except her, her good friend. Noa declared that she could not for the life of her understand why Dina had told all the girls on the Kibbutz about the book, but that she had had to hear about it from Mirale. "I tried to get more details, but you know Mirale," Noa added bitterly. "One would need to be a KGB agent in order to extract details from her." Noa went on to remind Dina that she told her everything, literally everything, about that crazy time when she was having a secret affair with Yaniv, while still living with Hagai, because she just couldn't make up her mind which one was more handsome. They were both such fine specimens of masculine prowess and they were both so well endowed, giving her long hours of sublime pleasure that she didn't want to part with either of them. The memory made Dina snort in indignation. Noa always confided in her, telling her all the sordid details of her carnal escapades with glee in her eyes, clearly expecting Dina to share her enthusiasm. It never dawned on her that Dina wasn't entertained.

Dina prayed Noa wouldn't lift her head and see her. She feared that Noa, in her typical reckless fashion, would say something about the book in spite of the busy hour and the listening ears all around. Her fears were almost realized when her turn came to put her groceries on the counter. Noa saw Dina and let out air in a long whistle, saying in a low voice, "Oh, it's you, Dina. We have some hot stuff to discuss, you and me." Embarrassed, Dina mumbled something about the inappropriateness of "hot" stuff being discussed in a crowded room. Noa laughed her carefree laugh. "Just remember it's the second time you've managed to elude me. Next time I won't let you get away so easily."

On her way home Dina tried to figure out why she felt so reluctant to show her *Italian Treats* to Noa. She felt rather uncomfortable with Noa's typical forthright approach to sex. When she thought of Noa's lascivious gaze falling on the cuties that had become so dear to her, she felt strangely protective of them. Maybe she feared that Noa's direct approach would turn her magical book into a pornographic magazine. She imagined Noa's crude remarks about the vulnerable nudity of her handsome men. With time she has come to know each one of them, what they like, what they hate and what makes them laugh. Noa would not even try to talk to them. She would probably start cataloguing them according to their dick sizes, as if that was the only thing that mattered in a man. She had always hated that approach of Noa's.

When they were teenagers, they used to hang out at the swimming-pool for hours watching the young foreign volunteers. Noa always made such annoying comments about the contents of their bathing suits. Where had she learned this kind of crude talk? Dina had wondered. No other girl on the Kibbutz dared to talk like her. No wonder she was already divorced, twice! No man could survive her constant poisonous critique of his manliness. Nevertheless, in her heart Dina knew that her evasive maneuvers would only postpone the inevitable, and that sooner or later she would have to surrender the book into Noa's greedy hands.

Noa sinks into her favorite armchair by the window and opens the book with a satisfied giggle. Dina, that foolish sanctimonious prude! Did she really think she would be able to prevent me from seeing her precious book? She has always been such a righteous hypocrite. She also used to devour the half-naked guys in the swimming-pool with her eyes, but she would rather have taken a spin on the torture wheel than admit it. Oh, God forbid someone suspected her of aroused sexuality. Even at the age when we started feeling there were areas in our body that made us feel quite wonderful when they were touched in a certain way, she used to give me that sour lemon face whenever I raised the subject of boys. Even when the other girls conceded, with some embarrassment, that they occasionally rubbed their "ginees" (that silly name their kindergarten nanny insisted on using, as if it made vaginas somehow cute), Dina kept wearing the countenance of the Virgin Marry at the time of her conception, declaring, "There are things that should not be the subject of public discussion." Of course it never stopped her from playing with herself under the blanket when she thought no one was watching.

Noa opens the book and starts flipping the pages leisurely. Ahhmm, I have to admit that Dina rocked it. Big time. This book is even better than I imagined after hearing Mirale's stories. Mirale with her imaginary lover!

Who would have thought she was capable of it? I have to admit the idea makes me kind of horny… The naked men seem so natural in this setting of serene, beautiful environment, as if it's a nudist beach. What a sweet dream! She has read about a nudist village in Greece and it looked too good to be true. If her account overdraft didn't sink her financially, as it threatened to, she would definitely take the first flight there to spend her vacation in a place where the naked body is the accepted norm and nobody makes a fuss over bare tits or a dick that is taken out for a breath of fresh air.

Too many times she has felt like the cultural attaché of an alien, advanced society here among the sanctimonious, self-righteous, fear-driven, complex-battered indigenous population, whose fears were all centered on the body and its natural functions. She thinks of an incident from her early teen years when she started feeling like that. She remembers putting up her hand in class, asking to go to the toilet to change the hygienic pad she was wearing because she was menstruating. A deadly silence followed her innocent request. The teacher coughed uncomfortably and pointed to the door, the boys giggled and the pale-faced girls looked at her as if she had broken a sacred vow of silence – thou shall never utter the explicit name, but call it 'that time of the month,' or 'female trouble,' or some other nonsense.

Her friends' reactions made Noa chuckle as she went out of the stunned class. Oh, how she loved a grand exit! Almost as much as a grand entrance. She was looking forward to the lecture she was bound to get from Dina and Mirale, her best friends, who would probably try to persuade her to use their childish nicknames for everything that had to do with the body. And Sex. From a very young age Noa used to feel a tremor of expectation whenever she thought of this mysterious affair that adults were so unfairly keeping to themselves. She was determined to unlock its secrets and spill them out into the bright sunlight. She was endlessly amused by the squeals of protest and nervous laughter that occurred every time she used the explicit words for sexual organs or sexual acts. It was so easy to manipulate the silly girls around her. All she had to do was say something like, "Have you seen Yossi's dick lately? It has grown hairs!" in order to get that satisfying, predictable response. Mirale would squeal and cover her ears and Dina would say reproachfully, "Why must you always shock people? You should say 'his thing,' or 'his package,' or something like that."

Oh, she knew very well all the stupid nicknames for that interesting organ that men carried so proudly in front of them. She could call it Bulbul, Zalman, Zereg, one-eyed trouser snake or birdie; or the ridiculous new names she learned from the volunteers, such as Willie, Johnson, baby-maker, meat popsicle and yogurt gun, but they didn't quite achieve the desired effect of the spills of laughter that followed every time she said 'dick' or 'penis.' She even looked up "penis" in an encyclopedia once, hoping to find some more titillating words, and found "phallus." This word really made an impression on her because it was connected to all kinds of important psychological complexes that grown-ups had, but nobody understood the word. They just gave her weird looks when she used it, so she went back to her favorite word, 'dick.'

During one of her visits to Haifa to see her cousin Nili, who was a year older than her and well-versed in the ways of grown-ups, they developed a new interest in reading the magazines that were hidden under the mattress in her uncle and aunt's bedroom. They took some of the magazines with them on their daily excursions to the railway tracks. Their favorite hobby was collecting flattened coins they put on the tracks to be pressed by the passing trains. They would find a shady spot, make a little camp there, and take out the magazines to while away the long, tedious wait for a train to pass. They eagerly read how the brawny arms of the tough looking secret agent grabbed the beautiful spy who tried to seduce him, turned her round swiftly and knocked her off her feet with a long, passionate kiss. They even tried practicing it but it was very awkward and quite difficult to reenact. Nili was very angry with Noa for losing her balance in the middle of attempting to sweep Nili, playing the role of the beautiful temptress, off her feet, resulting in a glorious fall on the ass for poor Nili. They argued over who got to read the 'good bits,' which usually involved 'sucking stone hard nipples' and 'thrusting engorged messengers of love into honey dripping tunnels.' At the time she didn't know what it all meant, but it sounded so wonderfully interesting and excitingly dangerous.

Years later, when she visited Nili during a leave of absence from the army, they sat on Nili's balcony overlooking the Haifa harbor, smoking Noblesse, the cheap eye-irritating cigarettes the Kibbutz sent its soldiers, and reminisced about those old erotic magazines.

"You know, in retrospect, I think those stories were most educational." Noa said, sending up a cloud of smoke and coughing a little. Nili raised her eyebrows. "With the exclusion of ridiculous nicknames for the private parts and the total bullshit portrayal of women who want to be penetrated anytime, anywhere, in any manner possible..."

"So what's left after those scenes are removed?" wondered Nili.

"Ahh," Noa said, exhaling another cloud of smoke, "the most important thing – the zeitgeist!" Nili looked perplexed and Noa continued. "I mean the sheer unmasked, unaculterated enthusiasm for sex! You couldn't help but get caught up in the horniness of those stories. I used to play them in my mind's eye when I masturbated in my bed."

"And you consider that educational?" Nili laughed. "Try telling that to my parents. They nearly had a heart attack when they discovered we had been reading their secret magazines."

"Of course it was educational!" Noa protested. "It was definitely better than the hypocritical attitude of our parents and teachers regarding sex. They tried to make it as boring as possible with all their so-called, scientific explanations, in the faint hope that we would lose interest in sex altogether and become celibate. Do you remember the lecture we got in the 8th grade from the school nurse? The girls got a lecture on menstruation, which the boys weren't allowed to hear, so they kept peeping in through the windows; and later the boys got a lecture about the changes in their body during puberty, to which the girls listened eagerly from behind the closed door. But nobody bothered to talk to us about the sexual urges that were driving us crazy with craving for something we couldn't quite understand. They weren't even willing to acknowledge us as sexual beings. I was beginning to think I was some kind of freak for wanting to have sex. That's why I found so much consolation in those dirty magazines. They confirmed to me that I was perfectly normal."

Noa looks at the smiling tanned youth who is standing in front of her totally naked, but acting as though he were wearing an Armani suit. "Look," he says, "you don't have to take off all your clothes right away if you don't want to, but I'd really recommend it if you want to blend in quickly. You see, if you keep your bathing suit on you will immediately stand out in the crowd." She hesitates for a minute, takes a deep breath, as if diving into an unknown pool, and slides her dress up in one swift movement. With her eyes still closed she takes off her bikini bra and undoes the strings that hold her bikini bottom together with accurate, decisive movements. When she opens her eyes again to see his appreciative look, she is glad she got rid of the shell of social convention, her clothing. "Welcome to our garden of Eden," he says with a wide smile, and opens the gate.

The beach is bustling with people playing ball, sunbathing and watching the surfers. A tall man is making giant soap bubbles with ropes dipped in crates of soap water, and a little crowd is gathered around him to watch. Giant soap bubbles rise and float lazily across the beach. The sea, the golden sands, the little white houses on the slopes and the mountains behind them are reflected in the metallic rainbow colors of the bubbles, making the whole scene surreal. She feels a need for solitude, so she goes toward the oaks and poplars that cast a pleasant shade by the edge of the beach. She has a sudden urge to pee, but the public toilets are far away, at the entrance to the beach, so she goes further in among the trees and bushes until she finds a clearing and squats.

She is so absorbed that only when she gets up does she notice the man who is leaning against a tree nearby, looking at her with an amused expression on his face. She freezes. How long has he been watching her? Being caught in this intimate act sends shudders down Noa's spine, but strangely enough they are not unpleasant. Should she say something? Should she pretend she didn't see him and walk away? The surprise of being watched while peeing throws Noa off her customary course of action. She usually takes the initiative and steers men in the direction that is desirable in her eyes. But for once she hesitates, undecided about what to do next. Sensing her hesitation, he approaches her slowly, his penetrating gaze steady and unwavering. Unable to bear the humiliation of him seeing her peeing, she turns her back to go but he grabs her arm and says in a quiet, baritone voice slightly tinged with a foreign accent, "Please don't go just yet… please."

Her heart skips a beat at the sound of his confident voice but she tosses her long hair with a proud nod and says reproachfully, "I think it's very rude of you to spy on girls who go into the bushes to pee."

"Sorry," he says in an unapologetic tone, "but I was here first. You were in such a hurry that you simply didn't see me standing here doing exactly the same thing. Come to think of it," He adds in a teasing voice, "I'm lucky you didn't pee on my leg."

Noa feels her ears burning. Almost against her will she raises her eyes to him, half expecting to see a sneering look, but she's met with a wide smile and twinkling blue eyes. He has a distinct Germanic jaw in a square-shaped face and very short blond hair. His wide chest is covered with a soft down. His biceps are quite impressive, bulging noticeably, and she feels the blood draining from her face, traveling south, where it starts pulsating in her pelvis.

"Are you new here? Would you like me to show you around?" He offers her his hand in a gallant gesture.

She chooses one of her most seductive smiles and flashes it at him. "With pleasure…?"

"Hans," he answers immediately in response to the question in her eyes.

Of course his name is Hans, she chuckles inwardly. She is reminded of the handsome German volunteer whom she was so desperately in love with when she was fifteen. To her great frustration he had proved immune to her budding charms and insisted she was too young for his mature age of twenty-four. It must be Hans, she sighs. No other name will do.

Noa exhales with longing and spreads her legs a little more to let her fingers find her already swollen clitoris. Rubbing it gently, her index finger starts circling and every now and then gently squeezing it between her finger and thumb. She relishes the slight jolt of pain that reverberates through her body every time she does this. Her breathing quickens and her eyes half close, losing focus, when she suddenly remembers that she is on the evening duty roster in the dining hall. "Oh shoot, I was so close," she grumbles and reluctantly gets up from the armchair. She closes the book, carefully placing a decorated bookmark at the page with Hans's picture. Patting it fondly she says, "To be continued, honey."

Hans comes to her in her dreams once or twice, but it's not until two days later that she manages to secure some free, uninterrupted time in the afternoon just for her and her new boy-toy. Unlike her friends, she doesn't have any small kids that have to be retrieved from the children's houses at four o'clock, the sacred hour for mothers. She can lie on the deep purple velvet of her chaise longue and let herself be carried away by this handsome stranger.

After walking around the nudist village for a while, she starts feeling bored. "Would you like to come to my room?" She asks Hans, and immediately starts walking in that direction.

He grabs her arm firmly and says nonchalantly, "I was under the impression we were heading toward my room."

"Is that so?" She raises her eyebrow at him. He just smiles, turns her around and walks her in the direction of his room. Surprised by his sudden initiative, she decides to go along with it. His room is slightly bigger than hers and has a nice view of the sea. It looks very enticing with its white walls and all white linen, set off by the dark brown wooden ceiling and floor. Through the wide glass porch door she sees the turquoise hues of the sea dotted with the white foam of the breaking waves. Hans lies down on the bed, patting the place beside him, signaling for her to come to his side. She smiles at the familiar scenario that never fails to ignite warm excitement at the bottom of her spine. He embraces her and lays her down gently on her back. Looking at him from this angle, his jaw seems even more angular and determined. She reaches up to caress his blond stubble, but he grabs her hand and gently puts it down by her side. Leaning toward her, he runs his fingers through her soft, long auburn hair and she moans with pleasure. She parts her full, red lips, waiting to be kissed, but instead she feels a light tug on her hair that stretches her neck backwards, exposing it for the soft trail of kisses that sends tingling shudders down her spine. It doesn't surprise her to see that he knows all about her secret spots of arousal. Next he would probably target her nipples, the soft skin behind her knees and the insides of her thighs. It's a sure trail of pleasure.

She relaxes, expecting to feel his mouth on her pert nipples, and smiles when she feels his warm tongue travelling down her neck, into the valley between her breasts. His tongue slowly marks concentric circles around her beasts, gradually narrowing, but annoyingly, never reaching the summit. Longing to feel him sucking her nipples, she raises her head and says softly, "Hey, aren't you forgetting something?"

He smiles confidently. "Oh, I don't think so." Suddenly, leaving her breasts altogether, he moves down to her feet where he starts sucking her toes.

She giggles in protest, "I'm ticklish there."

"That may be so, but you're not allowed to giggle, my lady, or I will cease and desist immediately," he says, sounding like he means it.

Stifling a smile, she tries to keep still while he sucks on her toes, one by one, poking his fingers between them. After what seems like a pleasantly tormenting forever, he leaves her toes and starts climbing up her calves, massaging them gently as he goes further and further up her legs. The tender skin behind her knees gets special attention and care, which magnifies her expectations. He starts caressing her inner thighs, first with the tips of his fingers, then with a full, flat hand and finally with his tongue. His advance is painfully slow and Noa tries to speed things up a little by taking his hand and placing it in the center of attention, the slightly swollen lips of her vagina. He takes his hand off and goes back to caressing and massaging, in wide circles, the area around her genitals. When she tries to steer him in the desired direction again, he pins her hands down resolutely, and continues the tour with his tongue, slowly licking, kissing and nibbling her yearning flesh. She groans with surprise and frustration.

"Enough, you're driving me crazy with all this licking and nibbling. When will you get to my breasts? Aren't they pretty? Aren't you dying to taste them? And my vagina is offended. You've visited the whole neighborhood around her except for her. Don't you want to pay her a visit?"

"Oh, my lady, my beautiful impatient lady, of course I'm yearning to suck your nipples and taste your lotus flower, but I want to taste your whole body first, to worship every sweet centimeter of your smooth skin, to see you up close, to revel in every sign of erotic arousal. You see, I have to map you out first, to study your body like a new textbook. I want to find out where you like to be touched, and how… Is it like this?" He asks, taking her whole nipple in his mouth and sucking it, "or like this?" Now he is circling her other nipple with his tongue and nibbling on it lightly.

Noa feels her whole body shiver as he touches of her nipples, which have become most sensitive by now. "Whatever it takes…" she moans, "I like variety and surprises. If you give me a box of chocolates, I'll have to bite each one of them just to make sure I'm not missing out on any of the flavors. So try everything, my handsome knight, be creative, and I'll let you know what does it for me."

"Just as long as you remember that you mustn't move. I dictate the rhythm," he warns her.

"So that's your game?" she says, and her breath catches when his warm hand starts moving slowly up her leg.

"Yes, that's my game for today. Do you like it?"

"If I didn't like it, you would have already heard about it," she tries to say but her words are swallowed by a sudden moan as his hand covers her throbbing vagina.

Noa gets up from the chaise longue with a sudden decisive movement and goes to get her favorite toy. She comes back with the sleek, pink, double headed vibrator, and starts it humming on her clitoris. She slides it up and down her moistered lips, ignoring the urge to slide it inside. She crosses her legs, tightening the pressure on the humming apparatus between them, feeling that teeth-chattering electrical buzz reverberating in her pelvis. Undoubtedly this is the best fantasy she's ever had. There's definitely something about that book which encourages great fantasies. She closes her eyes and goes back to her daydream.

Hans spreads her legs and starts licking her slowly, painfully slowly, from her toes upwards, all the way up to the meeting point at the apex of her thighs, and back again. He makes his tongue pointy so it draws a narrow hot pink ribbon along her leg. On the way up his tongue becomes a little wider, enveloping her outer lips and gently touching on the hidden inner ones, which stretch out a little in a delicate floral pattern. Catching them between his lips and pulling on them gently, he sucks and nibbles to her heart's delight. She feels her inner core temperature rise and tries to spread her legs wider so he'll be able to reach inside her, but he keeps a steady pressure on her thighs to prevent her from doing just that. She can't see his face but she can almost sense him smiling when she protests in frustration. He lets go of her lips and continues his journey back down to her feet. When he comes up again she is ready for him, catching his head between her thighs. He tries to pry them open, but in vain. She has always prided herself on her strong muscles, sculpted by countless Pilates lessons.

"I will let you go on one condition," she warns him, "that you suck me right here, right now."

He hums something incomprehensible in return that

she construes as an affirmation and lets him go, laughing at his red face.

"You don't play fair," he protests, breathing hard.

"Neither do you," she laughs. "I'm nearly dying here and you're toying with me."

He gives her a meaningful nod and dives between her legs. She leans back on the pillow with a victorious smile and spreads her legs as wide as she can, feeling herself opening up to him in more ways than one. He starts circling her magic pea with his tongue while his thumb slips into her moist crack. He inserts his thumb deeper, vibrating her clitoris with his tongue at the same time. Her legs start shaking and he knows she's going to come soon, so he presses his thumb into her and with a quick movement sinks his index finger into her anus. The surprise move makes her draw her breath in sharply, and soon the double penetration drives her higher and higher. He doubles his pressure at both ends and it's almost unbearably delectable.

Noa points the pink vibrator straight at her swollen clitoris and puts the speed on maximum. The vibrator hums like a giant bee. The stimulation is so intense she feels she won't be able to last very long.

Hans escalates the speed of his licking, while at the same time applying more pressure with his thumb and finger, moving them inside her in unison. The double penetration is her undoing. Her knees turn to jelly and her body starts shaking uncontrollably. She feels the waves of orgasm rising, covering her, and she's swept away, shaking and moaning unclear utterances.

Noa's hand is shaking harder than the pink vibrator. Throwing her head backwards, she revels in the subsiding wavelets of the orgasm. She is usually satisfied with just one orgasm when she masturbates, but this time she feels compelled to go on, to discover what else can be found in this addictive fantasy.

Hans lifts his head for a moment until the waves subside and her breathing goes back to a normal rhythm. When she's calm again he resumes his licking. Soon she feels the waves of passion rising again, but this time she wants it all.

"I want you to fuck me, fuck me now," she whispers in his ear, "I want to feel your hard dick buried deep inside me."

But Hans just chuckles, obviously pleased with himself. "It's not going to happen today, baby."

Noa can't believe her ears. It's the first time a man has declined her offer. For a moment her bruised ego urges her to get up and leave, but her weak knees betray her. Her craving to be fucked is so intense that her vagina is aching.

"I'm begging you, please…" her voice breaks down, "Please, fuck me now, fuck me hard, I need to be fucked."

His laughter rings out loud and deep, in his baritone voice. "Forget it, you're not getting any dick today."

He runs his finger around and around the throbbing entrance to her love tunnel, toying with her clitoris, every now and then inserting his finger forcefully inside her, which sends waves of acute pleasure through her body. She clenches her thighs on his hand, trying to deepen the penetration, but it simply isn't enough.

"What do I have to do so you'll fuck me?" she asks in a hoarse whisper.

He pauses to think for a minute. "Blow me."

She bends down over him, one hand stroking his soft, hairy balls and the other holding his erection. She caresses the head with her lips and then runs her tongue around the top and down to the base of his dick, feeling its silken skin. She opens her mouth wide, trying to take it in, but she can barely even take in the head, which is very red now. She spits on her hand, closes it on his taut erection and starts moving it up and down while still licking and sucking the head. Her burning vagina demands attention so she rubs it on his knee to the rhythm of her mouth's movements on his dick. After a few minutes she raises her head and pleads once more.

"Now, please, fuck me now, I'm dying here…" but

he just goes on laughing, his eyes bright with amused pleasure.

Noa feels she has reached her limit. There's only so much frustration and rejection she can take in one day. Before he realizes what she's doing, she pushes him down on the bed, mounts him, and in one swift movement inserts his hot erection deep inside her, slamming herself on his pelvis. His dick is probably longer than average because she feels him in places she has never felt a dick before. She loves the way he fills her, so completely and utterly compressed inside her. It's a mixture of gentle pain and acute pleasure. She starts riding him, riding fast and hard, fucking him relentlessly, appeasing her frustration at the sweet agony of having to wait for this. He responds to her by lifting his pelvis rhythmically, attuned to her pace, and every time their bodies meet with a thud she feels electrical shock waves spreading through her body, all the way from her toes to the roots of the hair on her head. On the verge of climaxing, he grabs her by her breasts and pins her to him so strongly that her clitoris feels the pressure. Losing all control, her eyes go dim and she hears herself screaming like she's never screamed before. Impaled on him, she trembles as the strong waves of an explosive orgasm sweep over her. Finally she collapses, exhausted, on his sweaty chest.

Noa pulls out the fiercely humming vibrator. It's dripping with her juices along its whole impressive length. While washing it carefully she thinks about the experience she has just had. She has never before indulged in such an elaborate and detailed fantasy. It was like being in a movie, like living a dream. She wonders where this scene of her begging to be fucked comes from. She still can't believe she wanted to be dominated, slightly humiliated and frustrated, but at the same time she can't deny the deep pleasure she found in it. No doubt, she giggles to herself, the meeting with Yaniv tonight is going to be different than usual, very different.

Lital

Lital Alkaslasy stared at her computer screen. She had been chatting with Sami "The Hammer" for weeks now and she had never found it so difficult to write. Shielded by the fine lace veil of her nickname, "Shanttele," she had gracefully flirted with Sami, orchestrating her prompting questions, her compliments, the subtle and less subtle hints. She was conscious of hiding more than she had revealed, like in the picture she sent him, which accentuated her shoulders and deep cleavage, the part of herself she liked most, the silky smooth swelling white hills, barely touching, holding between them the beginning of the deep ravine that carefully captured the eye.

She was amazed at how easily writing usually came to her when she was writing to Sami. Her fingers moved quickly across the keyboard as if of their own volition.

Once, she thought, writers put their pens or their quills to paper… "You should hold the pencil between the middle finger and the ring finger, Litali, and not hold it as if you're going to stab someone with it," Miriam, her first grade teacher had said reproachfully. But now she wished her pen to be a knife that would penetrate the heart of the paper, the heart of Sami "The Hammer," who was reading her words. She hoped to stab his heart and draw passion and excitement from it.

"My amazing Shanttele, what are you doing to me? I can't sleep at night; instead I lie awake and dream of you in front of me with my eyes open, so beautiful and gentle in my arms, and my heart feels like it is about to explode with the force of emotions that rise in me. Baby, I can't wait any longer. I really want to see you. Will you? Please? Meet me?"

There it was, in front of her, on the screen. The seed of emotion she had planted weeks ago was now sprouting a will to act. But was she ready? *"Yes, I will,"* she typed, her hands shaking. *"I really want to meet you too, dear, but I'm also afraid…"*

"What are you afraid of, baby? What could possibly happen? We are the same two people who have been chatting here every night for the past two months. I know it's only on a computer screen and these are just

words, but I wish you could know what I am feeling in my heart. You move me, Shanttele, like no other girl has before. I feel I know you inside, and your soul is so beautiful. Now I only need to get to know the outer shell, and from the photographs you sent me, I can see that it's no less beautiful than what is inside."

Lital bit her lower lip. The last words pricked her like the sewing pins of Sima, who was in charge of the stock of clothes for the Kibbutz members. Sima always had to add extra material in order to make the pants bigger for Lital. Since Sima's stock didn't hold any fashionable materials, just leftovers from old work clothes, Lital had always worn pants with stripes of thick cotton khaki or dark blue denim sewn along the seams.

"My dear Hammer, I feel I have to confess something before we meet. Please be honest with me because I won't be able to stand the disappointment in your eyes when you see me and I'm actually different, very different, from what you expected."

"Kapara (literally: penance, as if to ward off the evil eye), Neshama (literally: soul), I can't imagine anything about you that will shock me."

"And if you find something about me that you don't like? Something unpleasant? Even ugly?"

"What could possibly be ugly about you? Since I've come to know your soul, any shape that you are won't matter. *You'll always be beautiful to me. Do you think I'm not afraid of what you'll think of me? I'm not exactly a Calvin Klein underwear model… LOL…"*

The tears that rose unexpectedly in Lital's eyes combined with the sudden laughter that rolled out as if against her will and left a bitter-sweet taste on her tongue. Still, she wanted to be sure. *"You already know, dear, that I'm not what you'd call 'slim.' In fact the lower part of my body is very different from the top part. It's like two women were taken, cut in half and glued at the waist into one. You see, I have the Mediterranean pelvis…"* She hit ENTER and waited anxiously for his reply.

"My sweet little coward, if you had told me that you were thin, like one of those skinny models that the clothes hang from like a clothes hanger without any filling, I would have put my foot on the gas and sped away as fast as I could. I am all bones and sharp angles so I need a soft, full woman to pad up all that is sharp and hard. Will you be that woman? I truly hope, and believe you will."

While reading this, Lital stopped, trying to hold back the tears. She cried and smiled, frowned, bit her lip and then laughed again as various scenarios of her first meeting with Sami "The Hammer" Saada flitted through her mind's eye. Will this simple mechanic from Tiberias, who left school at the age of 16 to take care of his elderly mother and six siblings, become her "one and only?" Her father, the manager of the palm tree orchard, which was the main source of income of the small kibbutz in the Jordan Valley, and her mother, secretary to the factory's CEO, will freak out when she brings him home to meet them. Her sister, the coordinator of the preschool children's houses, and her sister's husband, the manager of the cowshed, will raise an eyebrow and make a disapproving face at this surprising union. They'll probably exchange meaningful looks behind Lital's back in the dining hall, just as they do every holiday when all the families sit together at long tables in the dining hall and she's squeezed in between their twins and her younger sister, who is studying communication at the Kinneret College and who already has a serious boyfriend who is majoring in engineering. What's worse, they are not the only ones who give her throat-clenching looks. There are also the piercing sideways looks she gets every time she holds or feeds one of the twins or changes his diaper. Some "good soul" inevitably remarks sweetly, "Oh how it becomes you, *mazel tov*, may it soon be you…"

Will it really be me this time? She almost dared to nourish a bud of hope. Sami "The Hammer" surprised her with his protective tenderness and the poetic quality that shone through his in simple words. He was a simple man, as he had previously testified, apologizing for his unpolished language compared to her rich writing. He didn't have to apologize. She loved the simplicity that rendered his words powerful. His "otherness" lay like a cool dressing on her open wounds and her exposed nerves from years of living on the Kibbutz. She has always felt different; she was never one of the "gang." She was painfully aware of the fact that her slow, cumbersome movement got on everyone's nerves, not just her mother's. But unlike her mother, the girls didn't want to hurt her feelings by telling her that to her face.

The six years she spent in the Educational Mosad – the Kibbutz's junior high and high school, were the best years of her life. For the first time in her life she didn't feel worthless. She was the one who always helped with the production of events, holidays, graduation ceremonies and class trips. "You have made a considerable contribution to society," her homeroom teacher wrote on her report card, and she tried to console herself with this remark rather than look at her low grades in math and biology. Fortunately she was admitted into Oranim College, where she got her BA in education. When she graduated from Oranim she expected to continue working in the kindergarten, which she of course did.

"O.K., here goes nothing. Let's meet tomorrow at eight o'clock, but I don't want to meet you here, neither

*in the valley nor in Tiberias. Let's go somewhere where
nobody knows us and we won't be recognized."*

*"Is Café 200 in Ein-Gev good for you, my beautiful
girl?"*

"It's a date!" She pressed ENTER and her heart
started beating faster.

Sami Saada bent forward to read the answer on the
screen and a broad smile spread across his long face.
Deep wrinkles led the smile from the creased corners of
his brown eyes, along his eagle-like nose and high cheek
bones, all the way down to his thin lips and pointy chin,
which thrust forward in front of him as if challenging an
unseen opponent. It had taken him two months of hard
work to get to this moment. For long hours he had slaved
at the keyboard, trying to find words that would move
her, excite her, after he had found himself so moved and
excited by her words… and now he was getting hard
just from the thought of meeting her tomorrow, the real
Shanttele, in the flesh.

He had made the picture she sent him the screen saver
on his computer, and every time he turned his computer
on, he pictured himself laying his weary head on her
wonderfully soft breasts, caressing them, squeezing,
licking, sucking, tying and pinching them. 'Hold on… get
a grip! Go get a glass of cold water,' he scolded himself.
'You don't want to spoil it all by moving too fast. It's

not good to be hasty.' He didn't want to frighten her away with his strange ideas. She's so gentle and sweet. He has to go slowly, unlock each part of her separately, lift the hood, race the engine a little, listen to it, and see where it needs fine tuning. Maybe a little engine oil here and there will do the trick... Come on man, this is a Mercedes Benz 300CD Turbo Diesel, a classy car – not only a kibbutznik, but also educated at Oranim! This is no ordinary Subaru Justy from Tiberias – noisy, trashy, too much make-up and lipstick, high-heels it would be dangerous to fall from, pants tight enough to show her crack, and narrow ideas of how to rearrange his life.

His best friend, Shimon, had given up trying to fix him up with a girl. "We sent you all the best girls, the best of the best in Tiberias. They all strutted on the runway before you but you weren't interested in any of them! This one had a flat front; that one was an antique model; and that other one, judging by the way she walked, had a serious dent in her rear. What shall we do with you? I really don't know…"

His mother didn't stop nagging. Sami, Kapara, Ayuni (the apple of my eye), Albi (my heart), how come you can't find a nice girl from a good family to marry and build a home in Yisrael with? What about Zaguri's daughter? Such a beauty, shining black hair, big doe eyes, a good girl, who doesn't go out with boys. She sits all day long in the grocery store helping her parents. She would make a good wife for you. And what about Shula's granddaughter from the municipality? Just yesterday she met me and asked me about you. Look at you! So tall, with muscles in your arms like your father, *Alla Yerachmo* (literally: May God save his soul, meaning 'deceased'). What a man you are! What a man! Who can resist you, who? And you? Are you doing anything? No… you act like you have all the time in the world. You wait, you shop around… this one is chatty and that one is yapping… What are you waiting for? You're already turning thirty, Ibni (my son). You're not getting any younger and neither am I. And my grandchildren, Sami, what about my grandchildren? When will they come? When I'm too old to pick them up? Sami heard his mother's voice even when she wasn't talking. His heart ached for her, for his father, rest his soul, who continued to lecture him through his mother, his apostle here on earth.

But what about me? True, everyone has been trying to fix me up with the most beautiful girls in Tiberias, but how could I date these dolled-up girls who hang on my neck with eyes as round as the full moon, who blink long, black mascara-laden eyelashes at me, trying to seduce me with shining blood-red lips and hinting, no, expecting me to take them to my humble apartment and do all kinds of things to them.

Sami could feel how much they wanted him to do that, be the man, take the initiative, take them by force if necessary, but how could he play the man in bed if he had never played the game before? This was the terrible secret he has kept locked away in his heart, guarding it from his mother and his best friends, who were all convinced that Sami "The Hammer" was quite the "tool," when actually he has never known a woman, in the biblical sense. With clenched teeth he admitted to his reflection in the cracked bathroom mirror: I'm a virgin.

Only with Shanttele, whom he has never met, although they live but twenty minutes from each other, does he feel that he can open up and reveal the secret that has been tormenting him for so many years.

"I stand before you today stark naked. I'm naked not to the skin, but naked to the heart, to the bones and beyond… You see, my dear Shanttele, I've never lain with a woman before."

A minute after he pressed ENTER he put his head between his arms and bit his lips, but it was too late. The message was live on the screen. He closed his eyes tightly, afraid to read the response line that would surely arrive soon enough.

Lital leaned back and smiled a little smile. So he's a virgin, this big brawny man! The contrast between his masculine appearance and this surprising new information excited her. 'I wonder which of the men in the book that

Dina brought back from Rome he resembles.' Lital asked herself.

Dina studied with her at Oranim. They remained good friends after graduating and tried to meet whenever they could, even though they lived on different Kibbutzim. Lital closed her eyes, trying to remember the handsome men she saw in Dina's book during their last meeting in the café in Tzemach Junction, a popular meeting place for the Kibbutzniks of the Jordan Valley.

Does Sami look like Antonio who lies, eyes closed, with the sun shining on the bulging muscles in his arms; or would he be more like Arno who looks straight at you with a hint of a smile on his full lips, his open shirt revealing a hairy chest, his jeans slightly undone, revealing a dark hint of his genitals; or maybe like Gabriel who was waiting for her, stark naked in a golden wheat field, his erection piercing upwards towards the high heavens.

'Lital! Get a hold of yourself,' she reprimanded herself. Here you have a flesh and blood man who is waiting for your answer, and you are fantasizing about those Romans?

When, after what felt like an eternity, Sami eventually opened his eyes and read her answer, his heart almost leaped out of his chest. *"I rather like that you're a virgin. It makes you very special, different from any man I know. I'd be delighted to be your first and to guide you into this magical land of body and soul pleasures. You will be my tourist. I shall lie down at your feet like an unknown land and you will travel up and down my body until you know its every hill and every valley."*

Had Shanttele been able to see Sami's face when he read this sentence, she would have known at that moment that Sami's heart tied itself to hers forever.

Lital parked the old Subaru she got from the car pool on the kibbutz in the parking lot of Ein-Gev. She silently cursed the car pool manager who had given her this old piece of junk. It could barely make 110 kilometers per hour, and now she was running late. Her heart was pounding so fast that she had to stand for a minute to still it. She smoothed her dress and made sure it was in place since it had an irritating tendency to get wedged up her wide behind after she sat for too long. She peeked in the car mirror to make sure the peach colored lipstick accentuated her full lips but hadn't ended up all over her teeth. Her auburn hair, which lay in soft curls on her shoulders, pleased her, as did her brown eyes, which looked hazel with the expensive eyeliner she had bought herself. Her nose was definitely too long, she decided, twisting it lightly to express her dissatisfaction with this coarser part of her otherwise quite lovely face.

She took a deep breath and started walking towards the small café that had inviting antique street lamps and a jasmine-covered pergola to welcome her. The small square tables were spread around the veranda and overlooked the small fishing port of Ein-Gev. The water of the lake rose and descended slowly in long, lazy waves of dark velvet laced with golden threads from the street lamps. The sky was deep blue, not yet black, and the shimmering lights of Tiberias twinkled from the other side of the Kinneret. Lital inhaled the intoxicating smell of the jasmine flowers and silently prayed that the virtual magic that had brought Sami and her together wouldn't wear off tonight, at least not until midnight.

When she approached the tables a tall and very thin man rose up to greet her. Her heart started racing again. As very tall people often do, he arched his back and bent his head forward, buried in his shoulders, the thumbs of his big hands stuck in his belt. Oh my, he's tall, she thought, and too thin! But no matter, I'll fatten him up. His face is a little old and heavy, I would never have believed he's four years younger than me. But what a sweet smile! He should always smile. He looks ten years younger when he smiles.

Sami rises up slowly, his heart pounding, afraid to believe that the girl in front of him is his Shanttele. After her apologetic explanation the other day about how her look was far from perfect and her figure was molded in a typical Mediterranean shape, he had imagined something much worse. Something like his neighbor Linda, whose ass was so big she got stuck in the aisle by the cash register in the supermarket and they had to move the cash registers on both sides in order to extricate her. But this beautiful girl who is walking toward him is feminine and sexy beyond anything he had expected. Although, admittedly, her bottom part is two sizes larger than her upper body, her gait is graceful and pleasing, yes, very pleasing. Her wiggling hips dance temptingly under the thin fabric of her flowery dress. She looks like a delicate vase holding the stem of her neck, and above it her face shines out to him like the center of a flower surrounded by the petals of auburn hair blowing with the light breeze. He wipes his forehead in a mechanical motion. His balding head has never seemed more exposed and his hands have always been a source of discontent. The black grime that has gathered in the weathered cracks and along his nail beds can never be scrubbed clean, not even when he uses special cream with a hard brush on them. How could he touch this delicate orchid with his rough hands? He sticks his thumbs in his belt and asks embarrassedly, "Ahmm, Shanttele? I mean, Lital?"

She raises her hand to him in what looks like an uncomfortable angle, moves her head up and down as if trying to size him up and says in a soft melodic voice: "Shanttele at your service, Sami the Hammer."

She lets him lead her to a chair and sit her down at a table. Then, as it sometimes happens, time elapses without her being aware of its passing, so sweet is the conversation. Questions are asked, answers are given, silences gently unfold as his big hands cover hers, and the air is thick with anticipation. Lital listens to Sami's stories about his childhood, which sounds like it was quite difficult. Her head is tilted and her face is softly lit by the candlelight. Inadvertently, while playing with the liquid wax that pools around the burning candle wick, her finger slips into it too deeply. She pulls it back quickly with an expression that takes Sami's breath away. He gently holds her finger, which is covered with a soft, white crust, peels it and puts her finger in his mouth. She smiles at him, enchanted by this chivalrous act.

"Do you like playing with hot wax?" He asks her with an incomprehensible smile.

"Sometimes I let the children in the kindergarten do candles drippings," she says, embarrassed by the change in his tone, "if that's what you mean. But you should always remember to be very cautious so you don't burn your fingers, like what has just happened to me."

"That's right. One should be careful," he says in a tense voice that deepens her embarrassment even more.

Sami suddenly realizes she doesn't understand what he is hinting at and he has no other choice but to open up the subject with her. He won't rest until he knows for sure whether she could be the woman of his life, his one and only, the only one to know all his hidden secrets. She has already passed one test with flying colors, and now he has to see whether she will pass the other one as well.

Lital looks at his undecipherable expression and wrinkles form on her forehead. The silence, which was a comforting blanket around them just a few minutes ago, has now become cumbersome and awkward. Sammy's hands continue to caress hers in a mechanical movement. Something flutters inside him, twisting his mouth from side to side ever so slightly.

She tries a different angle. "Do you like candles? I know someone who makes her own candles. It's really fascinating to see the process, how she mixes the colors and puts in dry flowers and leaves. One minute everything is quivering, molten liquid and the next it's solid." She looks at his face and her voice dies out.

"Yeaah," he lingers on the word, "I like candles, but most of all, I like playing with them."

"Playing?" She wrinkles her forehead, clearly not catching on to what he's trying to tell her.

He raises his eyes to hers, takes a deep breath, and inwardly he repeats an expression he has borrowed from her: 'To life or death.'

"You said you like candle drippings, but have you ever

heard of playing games with candle drippings? Grown-ups games?" Lowering his head, he doesn't dare look into her eyes.

"Grown-ups games? Sami? What do you mean? Please tell me. You know you can tell me anything."

"I mean…" He clears his throat and finishes the sentence quickly as if gulping down a big glass of water, "games of dominance, BDSM, domimant and a submissive. Does this mean anything to you?"

She pulls her hand out of his with a sharp movement. "Sado-masochism? Isn't that all those perverts who wear black leather clothes and flog each other?" She recoils. "Are you into this, Sami? You never told me anything about it. Ahmm, I don't think I like it," she stutters. "No. Not at all," she adds in a more decisive tone.

He feels his stomach sinking. "Look, I'm not REALLY into it, it's not the main thing for me, not at all, and as a matter of fact I haven't even tried it yet. Shanttele, sweetie, I'm not hiding anything from you. Look, if you don't want to talk about it, then we're not going to talk about it and that's the end of the matter." He is silent for a minute, looking sadly into her eyes. "It doesn't really matter," he adds in a weak voice.

Lital feels her determination wavering. Sado-masochism sounds like one of those frightening things that her mother likes to fling in the faces of innocent girls who meet strangers on the internet and fall in love with them. She isn't convinced she wants to hear any more about it. Maybe a more decisive action is needed here, to better express her feelings on the matter. Perhaps she should get up and leave, this moment. If he wants to be with her he should realize she is not that kind of a girl.

Lital gets up from her seat. Sami gasps and catches her hand. "Shanttele," he pleads, "please don't go."

They remain silent for a long moment. She starts playing with a strand of her hair distractedly, staring at the golden light shimmering on the black velvet of the Kinneret.

"Look," Sami starts desperately, "let me explain. It's not just a whim. There's something deeper behind it. Please let me explain… please."

Biting her lower lip, she looks at his deeply set, soft brown eyes, trying to figure out what it is she feels flittering in her belly. On one hand, she feels angry with him for surprising her with this BDSM concept, but on the other hand, this is Sami, her own Hammer, the one who has written her beautiful love letters, who has entrusted her with his most secret thoughts. This seems important to him so maybe she should just listen for a while and then make up her mind about it. She can always get up and go, however it wouldn't be easy to come back if she leaves prematurely.

"Okay." She sits down again. "Tell me."

"The Master," he starts in a soft, patient voice, "is the almighty dominant. He dictates the terms and he sets the rules of what's to be done and what's not. But he's not a cruel ruler, not at all! He mustn't overstep the boundaries of his submissive. He's a kind and generous ruler who understands his sub, knows his or her likes and dislikes, and does only what is best for his sub. The sub trusts the Master completely and utterly. He or she knows the Master will never truly hurt him, and if he feels that the game has become too much for him to bear and it pushes his boundaries too far, the sub uses the *Safe Word* they have decided on previously, and the Master stops immediately. This way it is safe and pleasurable for everyone."

Lital listens with mixed feelings. Her aversion to this strange, new world that slowly unfolds before her, hasn't subsided, but at the same time she feels a twang in her heart, a compelling feeling of *déjà vu*, something both strange and familiar, like walking in a dream in a foreign city, in the company of foreigners, but knowing deep down that this is her hometown and these are her family members. The idea of complete surrender holds a strange attraction for her. It sends a tremor of excitement touched with fear down her spine. She can feel a dreaded expectation and the falling of great walls, the relaxation and serenity that stem from utter submission to a force greater than her.

Later, as she is lying naked, tied to the iron bed in Sami's almost bare apartment, while he is running around feverishly, lighting more and more candles, doubts start tormenting her again. Suddenly she sees herself as an actress in a B Horror movie, while Sami, in the role of the mad villain, is about to abuse her in horrible ways until she surrenders her life to him. Frightened, she mumbles, "No, no," and tries to wrestle her hands free, but in vain. Sami has tied the silk scarves around her wrists and ankles tightly. Her arms are raised above her head, tied to the headboard and her legs are spread widely apart, one tied to each side of the bed.

"Hush, my flower," Sami whispers gently. "Have no fear, my sub." He strokes her hair in a long, soft movement that sends shudders of pleasure down her spine and his hot breath in her ear carries the words, "I'm here for your pleasure, my princess."

Her muscle tone relaxes and she allows herself to enjoy the flickering of his warm tongue alongside her body.

"Are you ready, my love?" he asks reverently, his voice hoarse with excitement.

She nods slightly, her eyes closed, feeling very brave for challenging her fears. The sudden burn on her belly makes her arch her back but her momentary pang of pain is quickly alleviated with a chilly ice cube. Again, there she feels a short burn that is soon extinguished with a chilly tremor. The quick succession of the opposing sensations of extreme heat and extreme cold throws her senses into complete chaos and she finds herself panting loudly. Her pubic hill swells and a slightly sour, pleasant smell spreads through the small room. The unmistakable scent doesn't go unnoticed. Sami takes a candle in a jar, half molten, and stands between her spread legs. He closes his eyes for a moment and when he opens them again he beholds her feminine flower opening up to him, with its bulging pink petals glowing in the splendor of the candlelight, dripping milk and honey. Struck with awe at the sight of her magnificence, he closes his eyes, afraid of losing his sight for daring to look upon this beauty. His hands are shaking slightly and his lips murmur, "Blessed are You, Lord our God, King of the Universe, who has granted us life, sustained us, and enabled us to reach this occasion."[1]

---

1 The *Shehecheyanu* blessing (Hebrew: שהחינו, "Who has given us life") is a common Jewish prayer said when celebrating special occasions. It is said to express thanks for new and unusual experiences. [1] The blessing has been recited by Jews for nearly 2000 years. It comes from the Talmud (Berachot 54a, Pesakhim 7b, Sukkah 46a, etc.) (https://en.wikipedia.org/wiki/Shehecheyanu)

A shrill cry pierces his ears. "*Shema Yisrael*, Sami, *Shema Yisrael!*"[2]

Alarmed and frightened, he opens his eyes to see a big pool of hot wax on Lital's thigh.

Later, when she lies wrapped in bandages on the white metal bed in Poriya Hospital, watching Sami running around the E.R., fervently asking the nurses to check on Lital, urging them to call the doctor on duty, there isn't a shred of doubt left in Lital's heart. "Sami, come here for a minute." Her voice trembles, but not from pain.

"Just a minute, my love, I must get hold of that doctor before he goes to check somebody else. It's like that here. The doctor won't come unless you watch him like a hawk and nag him every second."

---

2   *Shema Yisrael* (or *Sh'ma Yisrael*; Hebrew: שְׁמַע יִשְׂרָאֵל; "Hear, [Oh] Israel") are the first two words of a section of the Torah, and is the title (sometimes shortened to simply *Shema*) of a prayer that serves as a centerpiece of the morning and evening Jewish prayer services. The first verse encapsulates the monotheistic essence of Judaism: "Hear, Oh Israel: the LORD our God, the LORD is one" (Hebrew: שְׁמַע יִשְׂרָאֵל ה' אֱלֹהֵינוּ ה' אֶחָד), found in Deuteronomy 6:4. Observant Jews consider the *Shema* to be the most important part of the prayer service in Judaism, and its twice-daily recitation as a mitzvah (religious commandment). It is traditional for Jews to say the *Shema* as their last words, and for parents to teach their children to say it before they go to sleep at night. (https://en.wikipedia.org/wiki/Shema_Yisrael)

"Let go, you've already asked the nurses at least ten times when the doctor is coming and you've asked the matron to do you a special favor, promising her a free check up on her car. You've done your best. Now come here for a minute, I want to talk to you."

Sami approaches her bed cautiously. Sitting on the edge of the chair beside her bed, he buries his face in the palm of her hand, sinking his burning lips into her flesh.

"You probably don't want to see me again, and I can't say I blame you," his voice breaks down. "I, I just want to say…" His voice sounds choked from the tears he is desperately trying to swallow. "I'm so sorry you're here because of me, with this terrible burn on your beautiful white leg." Lital is silent and he goes on, not knowing what to make of her silence, but determined to apologize as best he can. "You were so beautiful in the candlelight, like an ancient goddess, awe-inspiring, that was the word that came to my head, awe-inspiring, and I admit," he exhales loudly, "I admit that facing your unbelievable beauty, I lost myself for a minute." He purses his lips and keeps his face buried in her hand, not daring to look up. After a few moments of silence he can't bear the tension any more and looks up at her, amazed to see her smiling softly at him through her tears. She extends her other hand and caresses his face, following the moist path the tears left in the deep crevices in the corners of his eyes, along his eagle nose, his high cheekbones, beyond his thin, quivering lips, until it comes to rest on his pointed chin.

"So maybe next time you'll be tied up and I'll drip the hot wax on your body?"

Ronit

One night I woke up. Not from sleep, but rather from the deep slumber of twenty years of marriage. Even though I woke up in bed alongside the warm body of my husband who was snoring lightly, and not on the top of a rocky mountain after a month of fasting and meditation, I was struck speechless. However, I was in no mood to get out of bed, butt naked, and shout, "Eureka!" Not to mention the sad fact that I actually hadn't actually found anything. That, in a nutshell, was the crux of the matter, I admitted to myself.

After twenty years of being happily married to a loving husband who was blessed with a gorgeous body that drew ravenous looks from all female onlookers, and a fairly active sex life that produced three healthy children, all I knew about the *Big Bang, the Grand Shazzam,* the ultimate pinnacle of lovemaking – in short, the female orgasm – was taken from the literary descriptions of heroines in romantic novels. In those larger-than-life love stories, the heroine often described the mysterious experience as a great tidal wave that rose powerfully, sweeping her with it, while she lay submissively in the thrall of unspeakable palpitations, surrendering to the twitches of pleasure that fluttered through her body. It all sounded so nice and poetic, but for some unknown reason all these aquatic descriptions did was remind me of the frantic twitching of the carp my grandmother used to choose for Shabbat meals, on the fisherman's board, a second before meeting their fate; and that image didn't exactly whet my appetite for the actual experience of an orgasm. Where have all the fireworks gone, I wondered. Where was the sublime feeling of the body and soul merging with one's beloved? That's what an orgasm should be like, shouldn't it?

I asked my best friends once, during an intimate moment of girl talk, what they really felt when "it" overpowered them. Tali, who was happily married to Tzahi (they left the Kibbutz the same year we did), a Karate expert, looked at me with glassy eyes and said, "Oh, it feels like a bolt of electricity that goes from your vagina straight to your brain! POW! You feel like you're going to die but at the same time you want to live forever."

Mirale, of Mirale-and-Eitan, who is known for her famous recipe for double cream chocolate cake, said in a dreamy voice, "Ammm, having an orgasm feels like you're so totally immersed in endless, warm sweetness that you just don't want to open your eyes and find out you're not really there permanently.

Dina, as sweet and beautiful as ever (it's such a waste she's still stuck on the Kibbutz), said with a bashful smile, "Well, to tell you girls the truth, before the trip to Rome I don't know whether I could have told you anything about it, but after the romantic weekend we had there and that special present from Yisrael, I think I can safely say that it's the one moment that feels so good, I don't know whether to laugh or cry and I want to stay there forever." (OMG, that book Dina brought back from Rome is all I keep hearing about. They're all talking about it. I must make her bring it to me the next time we meet.

Noa was the only single one among us. I have always wondered why she remained on the Kibbutz in spite of her professed disdain for Socialism. But I must say she uses the relative advantages of her situation very well there, including the fresh supply of young and horny Bambachim (young Kibbutzniks who work for a year after their army service to save money for their studies or travels abroad). My continuous questioning made Noa reprimand me, "What's with all these questions? Do you mean to tell me you've been fucking that scrumptious husband of yours for twenty years, yet you've never experienced an orgasm? If so, how can we explain it to you? It's like trying to explain what red is to a blind man."

So maybe I am blind, I mean, how can I tell? It's not that I don't enjoy myself with Amos. I like having sex with him, especially when he's in the mood to pamper me. He drives me crazy when he licks me all over and gently strokes my back, something I've become totally addicted to. I swear I could lie under his warm hands for hours, getting high off that delightful shuddering that crawls up my spine, like my ginger cat, who at the first touch of my fingers behind her ears and under her chin, lies like a corpse with her legs spread open and her eyes rolling back. She gets so absorbed in it that at the height of her pleasure she often forgets to purr. Who knows? Maybe this is the feline equivalent of an orgasm. Then when I see that Amos is starting to get tired from all the licking and stroking, I take pity on him and let him penetrate me. For a short while it's quite nice but then he starts getting more and more excited, shoving himself inside me harder and harder. At this point I start getting bored, although I feel this accumulation of pressure, an unbearable burning necessity, like an itch on my back in that one place I just can't reach. So I raise my pelvis and press it against his hoping maybe he'll reach that throbbing place inside me and put me out of my misery. It doesn't take long after that. Two or three strong shoves and I feel sort of a relief, like the aftermath of a power surge. He collapses on top of me with a happy smile and whispers, "I felt you coming. It was great."

So this is what an orgasm feels like? No big deal, more like a very strong sneeze. I really don't understand why everyone makes such a big fuss about it.

When I was Danny's girlfriend, before I met Amos, he really liked it when I sucked him off. I can't say I was thrilled, but he got so excited that it almost felt cruel of me to refuse him. At first I didn't agree to swallow it too deep because I immediately gagged and felt like I was going to throw up, which wasn't a very sexy thing to do in the middle of lovemaking. But then Danny told me about a woman called "Deep Throat" who gave men incredible blow jobs, the kind that drove them absolutely crazy, and her secret was a clitoris hidden deep in her throat. That's why she used to swallow men's dicks right down to the balls. That story had me worried; perhaps I was also a freak of nature with a clitoris in my throat instead of the usual place. That would certainly explain a lot of what was wrong with me, especially my lack of enthusiasm for fucking. I thought it was worth a try to find out whether deep throating would work for me as well, so I was determined to suppress the nausea and swallow it whole, right down to the hairs at its base. It was very difficult to maneuver the delicate organ past my teeth without biting it. That actually happened once with someone who really isn't worth mentioning. It was a very unpleasant situation. Two stitches in the E.R. at Tel Hashomer Hospital made him break up with me, and frankly I didn't blame him for that.

So there I was, doing my best to swallow Danny's big dick while neither being suffocated nor maiming him. Him trying to push my head down further when I had to stop for a minute to get the hairs out of my teeth certainly didn't help. Danny got upset and said that I ruined his momentum. Really! After all my hard work and effort, he had the audacity to blame me! It wasn't the first time I found myself disappointed and hurt as a result of an ignorant male fantasy about female anatomy, about which they apparently know nothing.

Deborah, who insisted on being called Debby, was my best friend in school. Once I went to her house so we could do our homework together and she showed me a booklet of erotic stories she had found hidden in her parents' bedroom. We read it excitedly, trying to memorize key terms such as "his rooster blushed and swelled up." I found this zoological fact highly informative. Apparently the man's organ stretches, reddens and grows a comb when it's ready for intercourse. Ever since then I had looked for this comb of the cock in all my boyfriends' private parts, only to be disappointed time and time again. A belated realization brought me to the conclusion that Jewish males probably leave their precious combs in the hands of the mohel who performs their circumcisions. I longed to check out the validity of my theory and tried to meet male tourists, volunteers on the Kibbutz, but unfortunately that type of liaison didn't come to pass and I never got to experience the pleasure of having sex with a man who was in possession of a natural cock comb. Only years later did it dawn on me that a negligent translator had simply translated the word "cock" literally as "rooster."

During another part of the storybook Debby and I discovered that the heroine, who was horny to the point of oblivion, once had to make do with a round hairbrush due to a temporary shortage of available men. Hmm… that's interesting, I thought. I also happen to have a round hairbrush. Heating up with excitement I read on. "She took the brush and inserted it slowly, deeper and deeper into her house of treasures. She moaned with intense pleasure as she felt each bristle lodging deep in her hot, wet, lustful cave."

That was a day I would never forget. My mother didn't understand why I suddenly volunteered to wash all the hairbrushes in our house, but she approved of me wanting to help with the family chores, especially since this particular task wasn't part of my regular duties. After thoroughly cleaning the brushes I chose the round curling brush, locked myself in the bathroom, spread a towel on the floor, double checked with my fingers for the right hole and tried it. I could just barely contain the scream of agony that threatened to escape my lips. Every bristle lodged itself firmly into me! Two weeks later I was still walking with my legs slightly apart. At night I used to picture myself tracking down the man who wrote this erotic book. In my fantasy I finally caught up to him, kidnapped him, tied him to a bed and stuck the round hair brush right up his rear end so he could feel every bristle lodge itself in the walls of *his* tunnel of treasures. Ever since then I have had no faith in the accuracy of erotic literature.

For over twenty years I've been walking around in the world with sour frustration over my inability to experience an orgasm. How is it possible that every bimbo reports having wild orgasms from every cock that happens to be passing by, but I am left wondering whether I'm really colorblind or the only seer in the village of the blind, the little kid shouting that the emperor is naked while the rest of the world keeps on faking orgasms?

So I carried on, pondering this mystery, until one day Amos suggested buying me a special gift for our twentieth anniversary. I looked at him in astonishment. He usually didn't remember our anniversary unless I marked it with red in his calendar and left notes all over the house for a week before. All of the sudden he came up with the wild idea of taking me to a place that had always aroused my curiosity but that I'd never dared to go alone.

Hiding behind Amos' wide back, I went through the beaded curtain into the adult toy shop, *Erotica Style*. The walls were laden with bright pink boxes and inside, behind the cellophane, were male organs of all sizes, shapes and colors. Not bad, I thought. I was able to look closely at a variety of penises and enrich my limited acquaintance with the anatomy of the penis, though I seriously doubted that any real man possessed anything like these shiny pink mutations with the weird bulges on them. More than anything, I thought, they looked like new species of alien cacti found on Mars. Suddenly I was seized with the suspicion that rather than being designed by a horny woman, these strangely attractive organs were a figment of the imagination of a man with a very poor understanding of female anatomy.

The eager shop assistant behind the counter volunteered long explanations about the esteemed traits of each of the plastic organs, but Amos could see from the expression on my face that I wasn't very pleased with the selection presented to me. "Do you have more advanced models? The kind that vibrate and rotate and stuff like that?" he asked the shop assistant.

"But of course. We stock everything on the market. You have your simple vibrator, made in China, not bad, costs only 200 NIS. But if you're looking for something special and you're willing to invest a few extra shekels for your lovely wife…" – to my great embarrassment he paused meaningfully and winked at me before going on – "then you should go straight for the Rolls Royce of the industry, our latest model, something really extraordinary, guaranteed to give a woman an orgasm in under two minutes. That's why it's called "The Orgasm Inducer." There's no woman on earth who can remain immune to its power to elicit orgasms.

Hearing these last words, I raised my eyebrow at Amos and gave him a look that said, 'You did want to buy me something special for our twentieth anniversary, didn't you?' When the shop assistant noticed that he had captured my interest, he led us to a separate cabinet with a glass window that was brightly illuminated. He opened the lock and ceremoniously took out a white, half transparent vibrator that contained silver pearls at the bottom. But what took my breath away was the little comb that grew out of its base! I couldn't believe my eyes. After almost thirty years of exasperating searching, I had found the ultimate male organ with the comb I'd been looking for! So what if it was made out of silicone and worked on batteries instead of being attached to a young, eager Apollo? At my age you take what you can get.

The shop assistant demonstrated the wide range of options, the various rotational movements and rhythms, while the pearls swirled inside. I couldn't take my eyes off the shining comb that hummed gently, not even when Amos nearly fainted when he heard the price. He tried to pull me away but I wouldn't budge. I was already under the spell of this magnificent gadget and I wouldn't look at any other kind. I was even a little angry with him for trying to cheat me out of having the experience of my dreams. After all, why should a measly sum of 1800 NIS prevent me from fulfilling the fantasy of a lifetime?

We paid and took the wondrous device home with us, our minds set on using it that very evening, but our plans were foiled by Yafit and Yossi, who came by to say hello and present us with a medal of honor for surviving twenty years together. If anyone knew the ups and down we'd been through, it was them. Yossi held one of the Chuppah poles at our wedding and Yafit had wiped my running mascara. We said 'Thank you, you really shouldn't have,' and they accepted it as an invitation to stay until the newsflash at midnight. After they finally went home we were too tired and Amos had an important business meeting early in the morning, so we went straight to bed.

And so it came to pass that I inaugurated the wonder stick on my own.

It's after lunch, and Tzlil has gone to ballet lessons and Shahar is absorbed in a 3D computer game. I lock the bedroom door and, feeling very festive, unwrap the rustling cellophane. First I thoroughly read through the instructions, but there isn't anything there about recommended positions for maximizing pleasure, something I would have expected from a serious and responsible vibrator manufacturer. There is also no explanation about the variety of vibrations or the ranges of strength and velocity. It is obvious the manual was written by a man; all in all it is as exciting as reading the manual for a toaster.

I carefully pull the shiny silvery wand out of its cardboard nest. I start by checking the buttons, exploring what each one of them does. The button that operates the comb is quite simple, yielding a gentle vibration that becomes stronger and stronger as you press the up arrow. The second button, which operates the organ itself, makes a loud zooming noise and the whole wand starts circling wildly in quite a frightening manner. WTF? What sort of psychedelic substance was the designer of this apparatus on when he conceived the crazy idea of luring a woman to insert this portable hand-mixer inside herself? Did he imagine she would enjoy it?

I decide to press only the comb button. I wet my finger, slide it inside myself and started rubbing gently. After a while I gather enough courage to try the magic wand so I spread the inner lips and point the device at the approximate location of my clitoris. I am very excited but try not to get my hopes up so as not to be disappointed later, as I expect to be. After all, "Orgasm Inducer" sounds more like a far-fetched, exaggerated commercial description.

Well, it isn't. Far-fetched, I mean. Every word is true.

After ten minutes of using the vibrating magic wand I'm stretched, half fainted, on the bed, my legs shaking uncontrollably and my whole body in a sort of general melt-down, like jelly trembling to the rhythm of the humming cock comb. I think, 'Wow! No, make it double Wow!' With the lack of more suitable vocabulary to describe my feelings during this significant moment, 'Wow' will have to do. Now I finally understand what Noa has been talking about and admit to myself that she's right: there's no more point in trying to explain what an orgasm is to someone who hasn't experienced it, than there is in trying to explain what red is to a blind person.

For a moment I lie there filled to the brim with satisfaction at finally knowing what it feels like, but immediately I am seized by other, more disturbing thoughts. What about love? How can the sublime union of my body with the body of my beloved happen if I can only get off using a vibrator? How can it be that the love of my life has never, in spite of his dexterous efforts, succeeded in giving me the mind-blowing orgasm that a simple battery operated appliance has managed to do in less than ten minutes?

Oy vey. This is the last thing I need, Amos finding out about this. No, he must never know. It must remain a secret between the Inducer and me. Who knows what inferiority complex he might develop if he knows that a simple appliance has given me what he never could? He'll have problems functioning in bed, he'll become stressed out feeling that he needs to satisfy me no less than the silicone dick, and when, through no fault of his own, he inevitably fails, he'll become temporarily or even permanently impotent. I'm petrified. There's no doubt in my mind that in order to save my marriage and Amos's sexual potency I will have to fake it. The first time we take this state-of-the-art device into our bed together, he mustn't suspect that it's blowing my mind to kingdom come. I must contain my ecstasy at all costs, no matter what happens to me. I'll have to maintain my usually bored expression in spite of the trembling feet and spine-made-of-jelly feelings I experience. I'll have to play it cool, like it's nothing much, even if it kills me to do it. My feelings are expendable but Amos's sexual prowess isn't.

I wait expectantly and apprehensively for Amos to come home but he comes back so tired I understand nothing is going to happen tonight. The same thing happens the next night and the next. Tzlil caught the flu so I have put her to sleep on a mattress in our room in case her temperature spikes in the night. Then on the weekend my in-laws come for their monthly visit. We give them our room and go to sleep with the children. On Sunday a new week starts with all the running and traveling, work meetings and driving the kids around for school and activities. You know the usual story. So when Amos and I finally find an hour for ourselves without any disturbances, I have already accumulated more than a few hours of solo flying without him knowing about it, of course.

The evening comes and we are alone. Tzlil is asleep, Shahar went out with friends and neither of us is tired. We silence the phone and lock the door, twice. I present Amos with the wondrous device. He peels it from the cellophane (which I was very careful to keep intact) and says, "Tell me how you like it best." I nod with closed eyes, silently chanting the mantra I've repeated a thousand times in my head, like a prisoner who is being taken for interrogation in a Syrian prison, 'Don't give in, don't surrender any sign of sexual arousal, no sign of unusual excitement, no moan, no tremor, no epileptic twitching. Even if it kills you to hide it, you shall prevail.'

I've always loved Amos's body. He has smooth chocolate skin, and even at the age of forty-five, his belly is as flat and firm as a board. I am very proud of him. The typical bulging belly of the ordinary, middle-aged Israeli male is even more repulsive to me than the remnants of ape genetics that express themselves in the thick back fur that most of the men have. I appreciate the effort he invests in keeping himself fit: gym practice twice a week and playing tennis and jogging in the evenings.

I find very quickly that those big resolutions, which were easy to make when I was alone, are not so easy to adhere to. Now that Amos, with his gorgeous body, is leaning over me, kissing me, licking me and vibrating various parts of my body that until recently have been enveloped in a deep sleep, I struggle to hide my pleasure. Every now and then, when I can't bear the tension anymore, a quiet moan escapes my lips. Amos is thrilled and doubles his efforts, trying all the various options of the magic wand. Knowing that sooner or later he's going to hit the right place and fearing that by then I'll be so exhausted from faking cool disinterest that I'll break under the pressure and admit my ultimate pleasure, I direct him straight to my sweet spot.

The now familiar tremors start climbing up my spine, but this time there is the additional stimulation of his licking and nibbling. I am already half unconscious, and my shaky legs are out of my control when the moment of penetration occurs and propels me higher than I have ever gone before. All I can think is, 'Wow! OMG, double, triple wow.' Amazed at the magnitude of the experience, I forget for a minute to fake frigidness, and that is my undoing. Amos keeps holding the flickering cock comb on my clitoris while penetrating me again and again. I can't be blamed for succumbing to this pressure. Under the circumstances it would be inhuman to expect me to continue faking it… Yes, I'm failing, I admit, but in my defense I can testify that no woman alive could survive the "Orgasm Inducer" without climaxing at least once.

I feel myself rising but I'm not myself anymore. Another woman is screaming her pleasure so hard that I can't believe it's possible. During all my solo times with the magic appliance I've never flown so high. All sorts of sensations are flowing simultaneously from the point where our bodies are joined together, to the far reaches of my body and back again, melting every cell they pass on the way, making me cry and laugh at the same time. This continues happening until a primordial cry is born from a place very deep inside me, a place I never knew existed. Amos holds me while my body trembles and convulses uncontrollably. Eventually the tremors subside and I start breathing again. Held close to his chest, listening to his heartbeat, I inhale his familiar scent and console myself with the thought that in spite of the humiliation of breaking under pressure, this experience has proven something very important: even with all the technological advancement of sexual devices, love is still irreplaceable when it comes to powerful orgasms.

A month later we go to the same store again, this time to borrow some hot videos. The friendly shop assistant recognizes me immediately and booms out, "Ah, it's you, the couple who has been married for twenty years. Tell me, how's the new vibrator? Good, eh?"

Heavy silence settles even more heavily into the quiet store. Three men who are browsing the shelves lift their heads, inspecting us with great interest. I look the salesman in the eye without blinking and say emphatically, "Oh yes. It was worth every shekel."

Ron-Lee

Surely there can be nothing more stressful than the first day of the school year, especially in a new school. I felt the sweat pooling in my armpits and prayed my new deodorant would be strong enough to hold back the flood. The giant zit that decided to arrive on this very stressful morning flickered like an ambulance's flashing light in the middle of my forehead. The yellow rectangular room with its big windows was packed with children who were all strangers to each other. We all tried to stealthily scan the faces around us. Who would be my friend and who my enemy? Someone let out a loud fart, unable to hold all that pressure in. Laughter and a lot of hand waving ensued. Who would be the first one to raise his hand and "tell us a little about yourself and your hobbies" like the ancient teacher asked, with a crimson smile that shone like a red sun on her cracked lips?

In the swirling chaos around me, my eyes suddenly focused on a girl who was sitting at the end of the second row. She glowed like a red poppy against the gray background. There was a special glint in her green eyes that was very much out of place in that barren classroom. Her thin lips were partly spread in a bewildered expression, but the proud twist at the corner of her mouth made it clear she would not accept any help even if it was offered. Her long, dark brown hair was brushed upward in a regal fashion, revealing a long white neck.

She was beautiful, there was no doubt about it, but saying it to her face was a terrible mistake, as I learned later. She thought I was being sarcastic and stopped talking to me altogether. I would be her magic mirror, I decided. Through my eyes she would see herself the way she really was – not a simple egret, but as a rare and wondrous bird from a distant, exotic land. Although she didn't seem impressed by my fervent words, she didn't decline to look at her reflection in the mirror I put before her.

Like Narcissus, who bent further and further towards his reflection in the clear water until he fell in and drowned, she bent herself towards me, and I yearned for the moment when she would lose her balance and fall in. I wanted to contain her, all of her, from her delicate ankles, hidden in heavy high-laced, army-style boots, to the top of her head, which towered above me, to that soft cloak of hair that draped me in lemon blossom silkiness. But all that came later, much later.

We talked for hours once I gathered all my courage and told her about my flying dream. I know I'm not the only one who has had a flying dream, but in my dream I was totally naked. The wind on my bare skin felt so wonderful that I wanted to try it for real, so I snuck out one night, stood on the lawn, took off my clothes, closed my eyes and breathed in all that darkness… But a minute later the sprinklers started working and I had to sneak back in, all wet, hoping that my parents wouldn't catch me. She didn't laugh at me, and I loved her for that. She just looked at me with that admiring look that melted my insides. Then she told me about her parents. She loved her Dad and it hurt her to see her Mom putting him down. Whenever she heard her mom calling her father "a lazy shmuck," something cringed inside her. She wanted to lift his limp hand and strike her mom hard across her pretty, smug face, to smear that red-hot lipstick, make it real for a change. Frankly, she scared me a little when she talked about her mother but it didn't diminish my loyalty one bit.

I only saw her father once and he seemed like a warm man, though somewhat absentminded. Her mom was an entirely different story. She was tall and slim with long legs that she made sure everyone noticed. She always wore elegant clothes, perfect make-up and bright jewelry, and she had long, dark red fingernails. She wasn't a beautiful woman but she was certainly very attractive. I once made the mistake of mentioning it to Ron-Lee and she reacted very strangely. Her cheeks flushed and she started crying. It took a lot of consoling and caressing to get her to tell me that she had seen her mother with another man. To make things worse, her mother used to lecture her about what was right and wrong in boy-girl relationships. She had this strange list of things you must never do, like hold hands in public or kiss with an open mouth. Kisses on the cheek were O.K. as long as they were not too wet.

I used to tease Ron-Lee by asking her for clarification through demonstration. Once she agreed to show me the RIGHT way to kiss. The touch of her soft lips on my cheek sent tingling shudders down my spine, very much like the ones I got the first time I listened to Pink Floyd's Dark *Side of the Moon*. I was so surprised by this new feeling that I just sat there and stared at her until she started laughing and brought me back to my senses. I snapped out of it because I could see that my strange stare had made her uneasy, but I couldn't stop thinking about that alternating cold and hot current that had overcome me. What was that all about? I'd been kissed before and it had never been a big deal, but THIS kiss... There was something different about it and I couldn't put my finger on it. I wanted to ask her for a demonstration of the WRONG kind of kiss so I would be absolutely sure I knew the difference, but I didn't have the courage to.

I guess Ron-Lee told me all those things about her parents because I wasn't just a passive listener. I empathized with her completely. Together we raged and ached, and together we were torn between these extreme emotions and, in spite of everything, the need to love. I tried to calm her fears with the power of my love for her and my brazen logic. Holding her tight and inhaling the lemon blossom smell of her hair, I fancied myself an armored knight, waving my sword bravely at the three-headed, fire-breathing dragon with the long, shiny, dark red finger nails. She might have giggled secretly at my gallant, though futile, efforts to save her from the hardships of life, but she loved me nonetheless for trying.

We were always together during breaks and after school. I often spent the night at her house, savoring the silence that filled the big, empty rooms. Her parents were almost never home and her little brother seemed to dislike being there alone as much as Ron-Lee did. He came home just for lunch and then went out again to play soccer with his friends. Ron-Lee wasn't her real name; it was the name I invented for her after she confessed to me how much she hated her real name.

When we went to her home we were often welcomed by Sara, the maid, who used to make the most delicious Kube (a grainy wheat crust filled with meat) in sour tomato sauce and white rice with crispy potato slices at the bottom of the pot, Persian style. When it was Sara's day off we went out for a pizza or falafel. My mother would have never dreamed such things were possible. She cooked our lunches daily and each of us (me and my three brothers) had our chores because "Mom is very tired after standing on her feet all day, cooking and cleaning and doing the laundry for you all. God bless you, you're such wonderful kids, but so dirty!" So the way things were in Ron-Lee's home was very weird and wonderful for me, just like she was. We were complementary opposites: me, with my excessive self-confidence, and the enormous need to touch, feel and understand everything; and she with her apprehensive loneliness, undermined by doubts and incertitude.

Our friendship deepened day by day. Our growing interdependency evoked some foreboding apprehensions in my mother's heart and she tried to persuade me to let go, even for a short while, but in vain. I was already addicted. Ron-Lee, for her part, had grown accustomed to drawing on my energies and I willingly let her do so. Her frail presence did not place a very big strain on my bursting, volcanic enthusiasm for life.

I wanted to know everything there was to know about her. I went through her family photo albums until I was acquainted with all of her cousins. I was surprised I didn't find many pictures of Ron-Lee in her early childhood. There was just one photograph of her as a chubby baby, dressed in a white dress, sitting on a beautiful Persian rug. Her eyes were wide open in an expression of fearful surprise, like she had been caught doing something wrong. The bright light separated her tiny figure from the big old fashioned living room, which remained in semi darkness, much like a Rembrandt painting. The strange thing was that Ron-Lee had no recollection of that room! That, and her feeling of estrangement from her mother, led us to weave elaborate speculations as to who her real parents were and why they couldn't, or wouldn't, raise her. The stories were many and the circumstances varied, but one element was constant: I always got to play the part of the trustworthy detective who, after many adventures and considerable risk, finally solves the mystery.

I became more and more possessive of her. Sharing her with her family was a necessary evil, sharing her with other students in school was a nuisance, and sharing her with a boyfriend, which I tried unsuccessfully to prevent, was absolutely revolting. Contrary to my advice, and completely against my opinion of what was right, Ron-Lee fell head over heels into that tricky situation called

Love. His light gray air-force uniform was probably the main cause of this unfortunate turn of events. He wasn't even a pilot, just a low ranking ground technician, but to a school girl who had never seen a man wearing that 'Whoa, I'd give anything to see you naked now' expression, just for her sake, he was a god. Add dark sunglasses and a cigarette to the picture... and how could I ever compete? A shiny motorcycle and you had the perfect 'Lady Killer' recipe.

I didn't even attempt to hide my resentment toward the new boyfriend, although deep down I was seriously scared of losing her for showing it. She tried to appease my fears by confiding in me about all her secrets, and I savored the most intimate details, not satisfied until I was sure she had told me everything that happened between them. I found some comfort in the thought that I knew more about their sexual encounters than soldier boy did, for he knew her body, whereas I knew her mind, her feelings and her innermost thoughts.

I knew he kissed her in the right way, but somehow it seemed the wrong way to do it. She tried to discuss it with him but he hushed her up by kissing her, again, in the right way. Quite a vicious cycle, I thought. I asked her if he had a lot of hair *down there* but she didn't know because they hadn't gotten to that point in their relationship, although he had managed to stick a finger in her vagina. She told me it was wonderful and exciting at first but that it started burning when he rubbed it too hard.

As I listened to her stories, I tried to ignore the gushing currents inside me and be the sympathetic listener I'd always been for her. It wasn't long before I realized that it wasn't Ron-Lee I was identifying with but rather soldier boy, who had done all these terrible things to her. This revelation shocked and paralyzed me. I didn't dare say anything to her about my mixed up feelings, fearing I might lose her friendship, so I went on playing the part of the loyal friend, sympathizing and comforting, while deep inside me roaring tidal waves rose and fell. Continents shifted too, and my world was reduced to chaos.

When she started telling me about the first time they did it, really did it, and about how much it hurt her, I felt I couldn't take it anymore. Something was bound to happen to me if I listened any longer. I'd explode, or break down or do something that I'd eventually be very sorry for.

"So why didn't you tell him to stop?" I nearly shouted at her.

She looked at me, a bit frightened, and tried to explain that she had been too embarrassed and ashamed to say anything.

"Why?" I demanded.

"Because he looked so...eager and focused that I was afraid to stop him."

I knew it would come to this and I believed it was all her mother's fault. She once told Ron-Lee that if a man got hard down there but was unable to act on it to the happy end, he would get the most terrible pain in his nuts.

"That's why those promiscuous girls who wear their skirts too high and their necklines too low are called 'nut crackers,'" Ron-Lee explained to me.

I agreed with her that being known as a 'nut cracker' would be the most awful thing, although I was sure her mother wouldn't have been happy to know, that in order to avoid this terrible stigma, her daughter took the next logical step and gave the poor guy the satisfaction he obviously needed so badly.

I didn't want to hear any more. I pretended I had to go because my mother needed my help. Back in the safety of the warm shower at home I couldn't help wondering what it would be like to be filled by a warm male organ. I started with rubbing myself, like always, but very soon got tired of this monotonous activity and went on to poking. At first it was only my finger, but the stimulating effect of that soon wore off and I found myself looking for bigger, fatter objects that could be safely inserted and gently moved in and out. In search of something more satisfying than my toothbrush handle,

I went to the kitchen and looked in the refrigerator. At first I examined the cucumbers. They had the right size and shape but they were all too cold, so I took a carrot instead. I went back to the bathroom, put a thick towel on the cold floor and lay down on it, with my precious carrot in my hand. Eager to try my new toy, I started pushing it gently inside me and then, excited by the strange and wonderful sensation, moved it harder and faster until I felt a soothing wave overcome me and the upsetting, urgent need to feel something hard inside me subsided.

Slowly I pulled the carrot out, took one look at it and nearly fainted. My carrot had been turned into a beetroot! No one had ever warned me that something like that might happen! I feared I had inflicted an internal injury on myself. How deep had the carrot gone? I wondered. Surely I needed urgent medical attention, but where could I get help? I mean, what would I tell the doctor? There was only one person in the whole world I could turn to. For the first time in our relationship, it was I who desperately needed help and Ron-Lee who came to the rescue. If she was surprised to hear my voice quavering with fear, she didn't show it, and I was grateful to her for that. It took her half an hour to get to my home, the longest 30 minutes of my life. I tried to remain calm and weigh my options: Would it be better to seek help and stay alive, but be forced to tell my parents and suffer eternal shame; or would it be better to bleed to death, bravely hiding my mortal wound, with my secret intact?

When I told Ron-Lee what had happened she started laughing so loudly I was afraid my mother would hear her. I felt the tears welling up in my eyes. There I was, mortally injured and the only person who could help me was laughing hard in my face. Ron-Lee must have noticed my distress for she stopped abruptly and then, ignoring my insulted expression, she hugged me, stroked my hair the way I liked her to, and very gently broke the news to me that I had lost my virginity to a carrot.

In the days that followed the carrot incident I hardly spoke to Ron-Lee. I just couldn't bear looking into her eyes, knowing she knew my embarrassing secret. I trembled with shame every time I remembered what had happened... The blood stained towel I didn't know what to do with, which Ron-Lee took with her to throw away on her way home; the laughter she could barely stifle; my embarrassment over my ignorance; and my fears... It was all unbearable. I'd rather give up masturbating altogether than be reminded of that scene. I'd rather give up Ron-Lee's friendship than face my shattered knight's armor. I di not feel like much of a knight anymore.

During the breaks at school I tried to avoid meeting her. To accomplish this I hurried out of some classes, and at other times I was late to lessons. I already had

5 warnings for tardiness that week. The vice principal called me in for a talk and told me he was not going to send a letter to my parents, but only because it was a very uncharacteristic of me, the star pupil, to act like this, but that this behavior had to stop. Nice. Easy for him to say. He didn't have to sit in front of her every day in class and see her questioning looks and the pain on her face.

In the end she caught me one day when I came up with the smokers from their hideout beyond the school's fences. I never smoked myself – I was disgusted by the awful taste – but I enjoyed sitting with them, smelling the curling smoke, sharing the hidden excitement of a forbidden cigarette. Ron-Lee planted herself in front of me and held me by the shoulders. I had no choice. She was a head taller than me. I looked down at her new wooden-soled clogs. They weren't the fashionable type, which were brown leather with decorative metal pins. She never succumbed to the dictates of fashion if it didn't suit her. Her clogs were made of stripes of light blue leather. I had no idea where she got them.

"Nice clogs," I said. "Where did you buy them?"

But Ron-Lee wasn't one to fall into such a cheap trap. "Stop it," she rattled me with a hint of anger in her voice. "I'm not going to let you get away with this. You've been avoiding me all week. What the hell has happened to you?"

"What's happened to me? What's happened? Are you serious? Don't you know? You're the only one who knows what really happened to me…"

She hugged me warmly and suddenly all the tears I had been holding back for a week streamed out. Not that gentle lone tear that can be wiped away with the back of your hand; I'm talking about a sudden breach in the main pipeline, a strong current that rises up like floodwaters in a dusty street, washing away everything in its path. I didn't know where to bury myself, so I buried my face in her sweet scented breasts. Her long hair wrapped me like a comforting silk blanket and if it were up to me, I would have died there, in her arms, embalmed in her dark hair.

The howling of the jackals from the Wadi pierces the silence of the night, fragmenting the rustle of her footsteps. It's Batya's favorite place for solitude. Whenever she feels the need to escape, she goes for a walk around the Kibbutz fence. That's the farthest she can get from the grievances of her relationship with Menashe, the pressures of her family, her work, her friends, the parents of the children in the Kindergarten who are quick to pass judgment, but only rarely give her a positive word. It usually takes only one round, but sometimes, like tonight, she needs two or even three full rounds to calm her inner storm. And for what? Over some stupid book? She scolds herself.

Every time her friends start talking about the famous book that Dina brought back from Rome and the exciting events that have occurred in the lives of the women on the Kibbutz following its arrival, she stares uninterestedly and volunteers to prepare coffee for everyone.

Unfortunately for her, Dina noticed it when they were on the beach by the Kinneret Lake and asked her directly if she was curious to see the book for herself. She tried to avoid the trap with a conciliatory smile. "Oh, I don't know, it's not for me… seeing naked men… what's in it for me…?"

"What do you mean, 'What's in it for you?' Don't you get horny looking at naked men? Doesn't it get you wet?"

Dina's probing questions made Batya, with her apologetic smile, freeze with embarrassment. In the past she has managed to put that question out of her mind and she hasn't confronted it for years. She thought it was successfully buried in the recesses of her mind, along with the bitter-sweet memories of the times with Ron-Lee that ended when her parents decided to immigrate to Canada. But then Dina awoke the memories with her snooping questions.

What now? What am I going to do with it now she asks herself, but no answer comes to her except for the howling of the jackals in the Wadi.

Sarah

Sarah looked out the car window into the darkness, trying to discern the shoreline of the Kinneret, but all she could see were some distant, twinkling lights. Probably Tiberias, she thought, since they were driving on the east side of the lake. Dan kept silent, concentrating on the narrow road. She tried the radio but couldn't find any familiar stations. It's as if they had vanished off the air, abandoning the evening to trilling Arabic songs and a strange language she couldn't quite make out.

"Do you think its Kyrgyzian or Armenian?" she asked thoughtfully, twisting a lock of hair around her forefinger.

"What?" Dan asked, startled.

"The language." She pointed to the radio.

"Oh, I don't know," he shrugged, "is there even a language called that – Kyrgyzian?" He was clearly perturbed.

"I-I'm sure there is, but I'm not sure about the pronunciation." She was clearly perplexed at his sudden annoyance.

"Then why do you do this name-dropping thing if you're not absolutely sure? Don't you know how foolish it makes you look?" She cringed a little, as if would help her avoid the icy tone of his words.

"I was just thinking out loud… people don't usually bother to verify their data when they're thinking," she snapped.

"Listen, Sarah." He softened his voice to a plea. "I just don't want to see you get hurt. We're going to meet all my old friends from the youth movement and they'll be watching you, so I don't want you to make any silly mistakes. You know how important first impressions are. If you start thinking out loud about weird things, like you often do, well, I'm used it to already so it's OK to do it with me, but if you do it with THEM – they'll laugh at you like… forever. They'll never let you forget it."

"OK, OK," she mutters under her breath, "I'll do my best to be as boring and predictable as possible."

They were silent for a while. The road started climbing up to the Golan Heights and the air became cooler. The darkness thickened around them. As much as she was looking forward to it before, Sarah was starting to regret agreeing to the weekend on the Kibbutz. If he's going to behave like that all weekend, she thought, it would probably have been better to stay home.

Dan felt uneasy after snapping at Sarah. He didn't want to admit it to himself, but he felt really anxious and apprehensive about what his friends would think of Sarah. She was certainly unconventional, with her playful spirit and strong self-confidence. She carried herself with the air of a princess. These qualities, which had attracted him to her in the first place, were what he feared could make the wrong impression in on his friends. He felt in the darkness for her hand and caressed it. Then he started telling her about a funny thing his professor had said in class the other day and the strained feeling between them evaporated.

It was late evening when they finally got to the Kibbutz. Sarah longed to stretch out on a white linen bed and let herself drift into a dreamless sleep, but Eitan, Dan's best friend, came to welcome them and said that all the guys were waiting for them in the Moadon (the members' club house). She was cheerfully introduced to the group as "The girl who snatched Danny-boy from Edna," and was left to talk to the girls while the guys were slapping Dan on the back and laughing loudly. While listening halfheartedly to the lively discussion of what work is harder, that of a kindergarten teacher or that of a cook in the Kibbutz kitchen, Sarah overheard bits of the guys' conversation and it made her prick up her ears. They were talking about their girlfriends' ex-boyfriends.

"Oh, you wouldn't believe how strong Noa's ex was. He could lift this table with you sitting on it!" said Yaniv.

"And did he lift you as well?" teased Eitan, and everyone laughed.

"No," snapped Yaniv, straightening his skinny, wiry body. "He never got a chance. I was too quick for him. He runs slower than a turtle with blisters on his feet."

"Get out of here!" said Zigi. "You should have seen Yafa's ex. He was as big as a refrigerator." Zigi spread out his huge arms to illustrate his point. "But all the lights were out up there," he snorted, pointing at his head. "There was no one at home!" The guys chuckled, but Eitan rolled his eyes and nodded his head a little at Dan to signify that the joke was on Zigi rather than the ex-boyfriend.

"Mirale's ex was nothing like that," he said deliberately, his eyes twinkling, taking another sip from his beer. "He's a fine fellow, a very good guy, so gullible that he believed me when I told him it was his duty as the manager of the kitchen to personally taste each and every dish. He has never forgotten the SMACK he got from Big Margo when she found him poking his finger into her chocolate cake…" Another burst of laughter filled the room.

"Ha!" Dan let out a short laugh. "He's not half the nerd that Sarah's ex is... a complete computer nerd, always working. He practically lives in the computer. So much so that whenever she wanted to have sex with him she had to e-mail him first to put in her request."

The guys shuffled uncomfortably and Sarah gasped. She had told Dan this in confidence and asked him to never tell anyone else. She felt a hot torrent of rage rising from her stomach while she frantically searched her mind for something to say that would hurt him back.

"Is that any better than you having to beg your frigid ex-girlfriend to make love to you?" she raised her voice and stepped toward the guys, who were dumbfounded. "If my memory serves me correctly, you talked of it being..." she paused dramatically, giving him a piercing look, "only once a month." All the guys looked away, pretending not to listen. "And that's when she was in a good mood," Sarah said, driving the dagger home with an icy tone. The cloud of embarrassment in the room deepened into a deadly silence. Even the girls felt something had happened and stopped talking. Sarah's knees trembled. She suddenly remembered that they all knew Edna very well and she was ashamed of herself for being so indiscreet. To her relief Eitan quickly turned the conversation to the work arrangements for tomorrow and the awkward moment passed.

On their way to the room that Eitan had prepared for them, Sarah spoke to Mirale with a tone of exasperation in her voice. "I'm so sorry for what I said earlier about Edna. I shouldn't have said what I did, but Dan just made me so angry! Why did he have to talk about my ex-boyfriend like that? Why does he feel he has to belittle him?"

Mirale just shrugged and smiled. "You know how boys get when they're together…"

Her answer puzzled Sarah and angered her even more, but she kept silent.

When they were finally alone, she berated Dan. "How could you betray my trust like that? Since when has my private life with you or before you become anybody's business?" She hissed at him, careful not to be overheard in the deep, calm night, whose silence was disturbed every now and then by the howling of jackals.

"I'm sorry, I didn't think you were listening," he fumbled, then dared to raise his voice a little. "Why did you have to butt into the conversation in the first place? It wasn't directed at you, you know."

"What do you mean, "Butt in?" Her eyes were hurling flaming pokers at him and her lips were trembling. "Can't I talk in front of your friends now? Are you that ashamed of me?" 'Nothing he says now can make up for this,' she thought.

"No, no, that's not what I meant," he muttered desperately, knowing he had only a few seconds to appease her before the final explosion. "Of course I'm not ashamed of you and of course you're allowed to talk as much as you want."

"So what is it then?" She demanded impatiently.

"Well," he considered his words carefully, "it's not always a good thing to talk. Sometimes it's better to just keep quiet."

"Oh yeah?" She asked sarcastically. "And do YOU know when to keep your mouth shut? I don't see how YOU applied this profound insight tonight, Mister Philosopher."

Dan bit his lip and shook his head to signify that as far as he was concerned this discussion was over. She's right, he thought. It was stupid of me to talk about her weirdo ex while she was around, especially when I know how sensitive she is about him. He tightened his mouth into a horizontal line and started spreading the sheets on the bed with violent movements. They brushed their teeth in silence, took off their clothes without a word and slept the whole night back to back in the narrow bed.

Dan woke up in the grey light of dawn. He took the dark blue, heavy cotton work clothes Eitan had given him and got dressed quietly. As he laced up his army boots he felt his spirits rising. He loved this cool, dewy hour when everybody was still asleep and it seemed like you were the only person awake in the world. He was going to work with Eitan and Yaniv in the apple orchard. They had said something about two blond girls, volunteers from Sweden, who worked with them. This should be interesting, he thought. It would give him a chance to brush up on his English.

When Sarah woke up she didn't remember where she was. She reached out to touch Dan but his side of the bed was empty and cold. She was puzzled for a moment, then remembered he had told her he would leave before she woke up. Apparently work in the apple orchard started in the middle of the night, she thought as she stretched herself on the bed. She looked at her watch. She should hurry if she didn't want to be late on her first day in the kitchen. She was worried they would actually ask her to cook something, but then calmed herself down by assuring herself there was no way they would let a rookie do the serious cooking on her first day at work. As it turned out her prediction was correct. All day long she scrubbed huge pots and pans and dived into sinks the size of a bath tub to retrieve all the kitchen utensils that were thrown into them without a second thought by the other girls in the kitchen. By the time they finally sat down to eat lunch, she was exhausted. She ate with great gusto, listening to the lively conversation around her, when they suddenly turned to her.

"So, Sarah, what do you study there, at the university?" asked Mirale.

"Umm," Sarah tried to swallow quickly, "political science and history".

"That sounds interesting," said Mirale. "Do you study about current political affairs or just about the past?"

"Oh Mirale, don't get her going, it sounds heavy and boring", said Yafa, and the other girls laughed. Mirale smiled patiently and signaled to Sarah not to take Yafa's words to heart.

"What year are you in?"

"Well, technically I'm in my third year at the university, which is usually the last year of the BA," explained Sarah, "but I'm actually on a direct course to a PhD. You know, when I applied, I had some doubts about being accepted. After all, they only let a few, outstanding students take a direct route to a PhD. Fortunately all went according to plan in my second year. I got an average of 98.7, and was accepted into the program!" She looked around, expecting the respectful looks and expressions of appreciation that she was used to getting whenever she told this story, but the girls remained quiet and just exchanged meaningful looks among themselves. After a short silence Yafa started telling a long, detailed story about how she had gone to Hanna, the head of the furniture committee, to ask for a new double mattress and how her request had been denied because as a bachelorette she didn't have enough points in her furniture budget for a double bed.

"What's wrong with your bed?" asked Noa. "As far as I remember it's a one and a half sized bed. It was good enough for Yaniv and me when we lived in that room."

"Ha," Yafa exhaled dismissively. "When was the last time you've stood Yaniv and Zigi side by side and taken a long, hard look at them?" her voice was slightly sharp at the edges. "OF COURSE you had plenty of room on the bed beside Yaniv; he's practically all skin and bones. But try sleeping next to Zigi and you're bound to find yourself on the floor in the morning."

Yafa should have known better than to open this subject with Noa. Noa flashed a quick look at her and said in a nonchalant voice, "There is only one problem with your argument. You base it on your vast experience of SLEEPING next to Zigi, whereas we don't do a lot of sleeping in our bed, so we do need a larger mattress."

A few muffled chuckles were heard and Yafa's cheeks reddened. Mirale tried to divert the conversation to a less inflammatory topic and said in a sympathetic tone, "Hanna is just being mean! Why can't she be a little more accommodating? After all SHE had no problem going to the Budget Committee to ask for a new mattress for herself even though it was near the end of the fiscal year and the general secretary said nobody was allowed to buy anything new until the beginning of the next year."

"Oh, I know," said Dalia. "That's because she didn't take it from the furniture budget. She got a letter from the doctor saying that unless Moishele sleeps on a special orthopedic mattress, he'll get a back strain again and might need surgery."

"That makes sense," said Mirale. "As head of the Medical Expenses Committee she must have known they haven't used up their entire budget this year."

"REALLY?" Yafa exhaled a long stream of scorching breath.

Sarah listened with interest. These domestic intrigues were fascinating. It was like taking part in a soap opera. "So you have different budgets for different expenses?" she said thoughtfully, almost as if talking to herself. "Can't you join the different budgets together to create one pool? It's the reasonable thing to do."

"Well", puffed Yafa, "it's all fine and reasonable in the academic world, but things are very different here, much more complicated than you can imagine, and I think you should spend some time learning about it before jumping in with suggestions."

"Chill out, Yafa," said Mirale reproachfully. "She just wants to help and I think she's on to something here, so you'd better listen to her."

Yafa frowned and it took a second nudge from Mirale to remind her to offer coffee all around.

Noa wanted to ease the tense ambiance by changing

the subject, and there was only one subject she liked talking about. "Who has seen the mysterious book that Dina brought back from Italy?" She cast a penetrating look around the table. "I've heard Mirale took it for a ride in secret," she teased. "Didn't you, Mirale?"

Mirale blushed. She was reluctant to divulge the details of her imagined affair with the handsome Italian but once Noa sunk her talons into you it was very difficult to escape. She told the wide-eyed girls just a little about the book, the men who inhabited it and how it had become her favorite bedside companion, but she didn't disclose any details about her Tony. The girls listened eagerly to Mirale's descriptions of the handsome Italians and bombarded her with questions, most of which she didn't want to answer. She was saved by the clock and the angry Moishele, the head chef, who hurried them back into the kitchen to finish the preparations for dinner.

Dan worked quickly, filling bag after bag with rosy apples. He kept glancing to the side to see how the Swedish girls were doing. They had their long blond hair tied back in rubber bands to keep it from getting caught in the branches, and he couldn't help wondering what they would look like with their beautiful hair down. He envisioned caressing their bare shoulders and perfect little tits, which were barely visible through the hard cotton of their work shirts. He woke up from his daydreaming to discover, to his dismay, that the girls had filled almost an entire crate by themselves while he was still struggling with the first bag. He bit his lips and doubled his efforts. He couldn't let them beat him. What would his friends say?! His stomach started rumbling as the sun got hotter, and he was thankful when Eitan called everyone to the little shed where they had their breakfast. When they finished eating the girls washed the dishes and the guys went out to smoke a cigarette.

The conversation wound its way around to the expected profit from the apples this year, then on to the rise in water costs, and got quite heated around the latest debate about the merging of the different budgets for the members of the Kibbutz.

"So how do you like Sarah?" asked Dan nonchalantly.

"Why do you want to know?" asked Zigi in mock surprise. "We're not the ones sleeping with her."

"I think she's great," said Eitan gallantly. "She's funny and smart, maybe too smart for her own good. I doubt you'll be able to sustain a relationship with someone who outsmarts you. Whenever you and I used to argue and I came up with a winning argument that you couldn't find an answer to, you got so angry that you turned red and offered to race me around the block. You knew I could never outrun you, so that calmed you down."

"That was years ago, when we were kids," protested Dan.

"She's quite cute." Zigi landed his remark in a deep baritone. "Sexy ass, decent tits…"

"Hey! Watch it, buddy! That's my girlfriend you're talking about," said Dan, elbowing Zigi, but his elbow didn't seem to make any indentation in Zigi's massive chest, and he just went on uninterrupted, "… but frankly you can have her. She's not woman enough for me."

"What do you mean?" snapped Dan. "You just said she's sexy."

"Oh, it's not about being sexy", said Zigi slowly, "it's more about knowing how to be a woman around your man… you know… all soft and warm, making cute little noises when you tickle her back, looking up to you… I don't see Sarah being like that. She's the bossy type, she's more…" he seemed at a loss for the right words.

"Sharp around the edges?" suggested Dan.

"Yeah, man." Zigi was relieved. "Exactly".

Waking from a long and satisfying slumber in the afternoon, Sarah wonders why Dan hasn't come back from the orchard yet. Shouldn't he be back since he left so early in the morning? But clearly working hours on the Kibbutz follow a different set of rules than the rest of the world, as Yafa had so graciously informed her. For a moment she feels apprehensive when she considers

Dan's reaction when he hears about the conversation from that morning. He would probably hear about it from Zigi, who would hear every little detail from Yafa, or from Eitan, who would be informed by Mirale. She remembers how angry she was with him the day before and decides she doesn't care if all his stupid friends hate her or not. As far as she's concerned they can all stand in line to kiss her shiny behind… She giggles when she remembers her grandma using that colorful figure of speech while talking about their religious neighbors, those "shwartze hayes" ("black animals" in Yiddish) who were appalled when grandma put a Strauss record on the gramophone on Friday nights and danced the waltz with grandpa. The thought of her grandma cheers her up and she starts getting dressed, humming the *Blue Danube* when Dan comes in looking pensive.

"Hi," she says nonchalantly, avoiding his eyes.

He's relieved to see her in a better mood than he expected. "Hi," he replies cautiously, "I'm sorry about yesterday. Can we forget it ever happened?"

"Well," she says, turning around to look at him. She drags out her answer. "It depends… What are you willing to do to make me forget?"

"What is your heart set on?" he smiles, recognizing her game. "Money? Power? Have pity, Madam. Remember I'm just a poor student."

She examines him closely as he takes off his mud-soiled clothes and stretches out his bare arms. "Hey you," she smiles mischievously. "I'm sure you can think of a way to make me forget..."

His smile widens. Watching her as she looks intensely at his half naked body sends a warm tingling sensation spiraling through his body. "You just hold that thought while I take a quick shower," he instructs her, "and you better get rid of your clothes... You won't be needing them where I'm going to take you."

"Oh no, Mister," she grabs his arm. "You're not going to abandon a damsel in distress, are you?"

His smile widens even further as he turns back to her. She is already unbuttoning his mud-soiled, dark blue trousers. "So... it's going to be like this then," he murmurs.

"Just" – down come the trousers – "Like" – down come the grey work underwear – "This," she says. Still laughing, she closes her fingers gently on his already erect member, which blushes with anticipation. He groans and closes his eyes. Her talent for giving a good blow job is unsurpassed. She can make him come in a few minutes if she wants to, or she can make him sustain his erection for as long as she wants it... and that afternoon she clearly wants him badly. He flings her on the bed eagerly, but she swiftly turns around, her face buried in his genitals, directing his mouth to her sweet spot. They don't need words. After years of love-making they know how to strum on each other's bodies to create that heavenly harmony of mutual sexual arousal.

He starts drawing circles on her outer lips with the tip of his tongue, slowly going round and round, paying an occasional visit to her clit, until he sees her pink button becoming moistened and fluttering with anticipation. He softens his tongue and continues circling it with a soft, warm, wet tongue, which extracts deep moans of pleasure from Sarah. Gradually, the circles become more and more focused on the inner petals of her beautiful lotus flower, occasionally invading the lovely, bright pink tunnel in its center. Every now and then he returns to her now protruding pleasure button and gives it a quick vibration with the tip of his tongue. Her groans become more and more audible and she even stops sucking his organ for fear of hurting him in the turmoil of her intense pleasure. He knows it means she is close, very close, to reaching climax, so he keeps on licking vigorously. When her legs start trembling he goes straight to her love button and sucks it as if he were sucking a delicious oyster out of its shell. Her groans become high pitched squeals, her whole body is shaking now, and he knows that in a minute she's going to pull him up to her with a dreamy smile to thank him for an "earthquake orgasm". And so she does.

The next day Sarah and Dan leave the Kibbutz after breakfast. They go to Mitzpe Hashalom in Kfar Haruv, where they can take in the whole Kinneret in one long glance. The strong eastern wind has an icy edge to it. Sarah shudders and presses herself against Dan's chest.

"It was very interesting, the visit to your Kibbutz. Everything is so different there. All in all I had a good time and I liked your friends, well, at least some of them."

Dan tightens his hug around her. "I'm glad you did."

"What did they say about me? Did you get their consent?" she asks, half joking, half serious.

He is silent for a moment, then clears his throat and says, "Hmm."

"Is this an approving 'Hmm' or a disapproving one?" she wonders.

"It depends on whom you ask," he answers reluctantly.

"Well?" she says impatiently, "spill it out already. They must have talked about me and I want you to tell me everything they said."

"O.K. So Eitan thinks you're cool. He said you're very intelligent and fun to be with, but I don't know how much his assessment is worth because he also said you're far too smart for me."

"Really? That's what he said? Oh, you know that's bullshit." She emits a short laugh. "He probably just wanted to tease you. He knows how important it is for you to get high marks this year, especially if you want to get an above 90 average, which would put you on the Dean's list of excellence."

"Zigi, on the other hand, thinks you're condescending and not very feminine. 'Sharp around the edges,' I believe was the phrase he used."

"What?" she shrieks, and adds after a momentary pause, "well, I guess he's the type of guy that checks a girl's front balcony before he decides to enter her apartment. Yafa is probably an E cup, maybe even an F, so of course my humble C is no match for hers."

"What?!" blurts Dan. "What ARE you talking about? Who said anything about tits? And you blame men for looking only at your breasts! Believe me, what he's talking about has nothing to do with your beautiful, quite sufficient breasts."

"Then what is it?" she asks irritably. "What's not feminine about me?"

"Don't get annoyed because of Zigi," Dan comforts her. "It's not worth it. He's just a big, rather thick-headed macho man who prefers women with small minds and big, adoring eyes."

"But you don't," she is half asking, half stating.

He kisses her frozen nose, "But I don't. I prefer you."

Yisrael

When people see Dina and me they often think she's much younger than I am, when in fact we are exactly the same age. She's fortunate that way. She looks as if the years haven't left their mark on her, and if you ask me, she's much hotter than any twenty-year-old chick with a belly revealing T-shirt, who has no concept about what a real woman looks like. Not a scrawny model, but not too fat either. A woman should be soft and curvy, with a narrow waist you can put your arm around; big, full, round breasts; and an ass you can grab hold of. I love Dina's breasts. Even though she breastfed our three children, her tits still look beautiful, supple and full, not like the empty milk bags I see on some of her friends. I love the feeling of her hardening nipples in my mouth and I love to grab hold of her tight, sexy ass and pull it hard against me when we're making love. Ah, that ass that she's spent countless Pilates hours shaping. It can drive a man crazy.

She goes to her folk dancing and works out three times a week, while I stay at home with the children, but I don't mind because I know she loves it and I love to see what it does to her ass, and her thighs... those strong thighs that grip me like pliers or tighten around my dick when I penetrate her from behind, doggy style. I feel her ass pressing against me, soft, smooth and flexible, that ass that attracts so many men's stares, like a magnet collects iron dust. When I see the way they drool over her ass it makes me wanna smash their faces. That perfect ass that draws beautiful circles in the air when she walks, or dances... Little does it know of the fire it ignites in men's loins. That sweet ass with its two round cheeks, smiling to the world, that ass raises my cannon every time I look at her.

We've been married for fifteen years and I know what people say, that after so many years you start getting bored in bed and start to look elsewhere, but not me. I've never looked at another woman in that way, except for my wife. That's how it's been, right from the start, from the eighth grade when we sat together at the first table near the window. I've always only had eyes for her. I've never loved another woman.

If I had gone the whole world round looking for a wife, I wouldn't have found a better or more perfect woman than her. She's the best mother to our children. She notices everything that happens to them, she is attentive to all their needs and they're the most important thing in the world to her. She's a good housewife, and it's no less important because we live on a Kibbutz. She has to take care of the laundry, make sure it is dropped off and picked up on time so I'll have a clean, freshly pressed shirt. She takes time to bake a cake for Shabbat and to have a hot meal ready for me when I come back dead tired from a long day of driving for the factory. She keeps the house tidy so we can invite friends over. She does all the little things that make a house a home. She's also my best friend. I can tell her everything I'm going through with the pressure at work and be certain she'll always back me one hundred percent.

She's been going on about how much she wants a romantic vacation, just the two of us, without the children – who are the light of my life, but it's true that they never allow us a moment alone to ourselves. Who can make love when they wake up crying from a bad dream or jump into your bed at 6:00 a.m.? She wants it to be just the two of us, without the Kibbutz, the members' meetings, the factory's board meetings, and all the chores that are waiting to be done, without the wagging tongues looking for juicy gossip. Just the two of us, anonymous, in the big, wide world.

I decided that Dina was right. In spite of our tight budget we owed it to ourselves. Just a short vacation, Sunday to Thursday, but it took all my organizational skills to make it happen. I had to pull a few strings, call in a few favors, and coordinate the many details. It wasn't easy, but I managed to sort it all out. First I had to bribe our babysitter, Neta, with the prospect of a car for the weekend at the factory's expense. Then I had to jump through hoops in order to postpone all the important meetings in the factory until the week after our vacation. The most difficult task was dealing with the sour faced principal of the school where Dina teaches. The principal tried to turn down my request with the feeble excuse that the Ministry of Education doesn't allow teachers to go abroad in the middle of the school year. It took a few calls and the application of moderate physical pressure to make her understand that if she wanted to have the *Family Book Party*, which Dina was in charge of organizing, on our Kibbutz, with funding from the factory, she had better do her best to keep Dina happy. Everything worked out well in the end. I was able to keep my promise to Dina and on a chilly spring evening we took off for Rome.

Of course she dragged me to all the famous sites written in her *Tourist Guide to Classic Rome*. It was tiring, not exactly my idea of a romantic vacation in Rome, but on the other hand, visiting Rome without seeing the Coloseum, which looks like a half-eaten wedding cake, or without breaking your neck below Michelangelo's ceiling in the Vatican, is simply unthinkable. We were very lucky to have rain on the second day so we could stop running around like poisoned rats in the streets. Instead we stayed in bed until late morning and then treated ourselves to breakfast in one of those lovely little cafés where you can assemble your own pizza with all the toppings you can think of. Then we just strolled leisurely, admiring the fancy dressed doormen at the entrances to the hotels along the street. They looked like soldiers in Napoleon Bonaparte's army. When the rain turned from a nice drizzle to a heavy shower, we found shelter in a weird little bookstore that was located in a caravan in the middle of the street.

I headed toward the shelf of picture books of Rome in order to see how many sites we still had to cover, and Dina went to browse the art section. She opened a big book and started flipping through the pages. A few minutes had gone by before I noticed she was still stuck on the same book. I went to see what was so interesting but as soon as she felt me behind her she closed the book abruptly, as if she didn't want me to see what was inside. Of course it only made me more curious and when I noticed that she was blushing, I got suspicious. My Dina has always been shy about certain matters. She turns red when the guys tell dirty jokes or when they put a pornographic movie on at the members' club, just for laughs.

I tore the book out of her hand almost forcefully. I had to see what had made her blush. There was a naked guy on the cover. He was smiling happily while sitting butt naked in a wheat field. For his sake I hoped they had let him keep his underwear on for the photo shoot. Wheat has long, hairy spikes on the grain heads that attach themselves to the hairs on your legs and really itch and irritate. That's why the Falachim (the field workers) always wear long trousers to work. When some naïve volunteer goes into the field with short pants, he always regrets it for weeks afterwards.

At first I thought it was an artistic book of nudes in nature, like the one she once showed me of a married couple who took nude pictures of each other in beautiful scenic locations around the world. I wasn't prepared for what I saw inside – naked men in positions I wouldn't be caught dead in, all exposed in the commander hatch, their erections sky high…. I saw the poor guy from the wheat field had had to lose his underwear after all. I gave Dina a questioning look. She turned red as a beetroot and lowered her head, the poor, sweet girl. I'd never have guessed she'd have the guts to pick up a book like this.

Then another thought hit me. If it turns her on, why not take it? So I bought it for her as a special gift. It was well worth the thirty Euros I paid for it just to see the admiring look on her face.

In the cab back to the hotel I couldn't take my hands off her. I saw the driver sneaking looks in the rearview mirror and smiling. Dina freaked out a little but I told her he must have seen dozens of couples like that every day. "Besides," I added, intoxicated by the feeling of anonymity, "we don't know this guy, he doesn't know anything about us, and we're in freaking Rome! So who cares what the Romans think of us?" It made her laugh and she calmed down a little.

"Still, I'd like to wait until we get to the hotel," she breathed hotly in my ear and threw in a 360-degree lick around my earlobe. That was literally below the belt. She knew perfectly well what it would do to me.

"And then what?" I whispered back and planted a wet kiss on the nape of her neck.

"I'll make the waiting worth your while… don't you worry, Mister," she added in her bedroom voice. I felt the pressure building up in my pants as she put her warm hand above my caged dick, which wished more than anything to get its head out into the open air.

When we finally got to our room, after waiting forever for the slow elevator to arrive and then having to endure the company of a fat, overly friendly American couple, I locked the door behind me and turned around to her, all eager to start. But then she did something she had never done before. She pushed me down on the bed and said in an unusually assertive voice, "Oh no, you're not doing anything now, honey. You're just watching."

Clearly she had some sort of premeditated plan, so I leaned back and waited curiously for the show. And Baam! What a show it was! She put the TV on the MTV channel and danced before me like a professional stripper, one who's used to dancing on poles and such, only she was doing it for me alone. I looked at her, fascinated, and suddenly she seemed like a stranger to me, but this strangeness only turned me on even more. I'd never be able to pluck up the courage to hit on an erotic dancer in a shady night club, but here I had my very own private erotic dancer!

She slowly unbuttoned her blouse, started playing with her beautiful breasts, moistened her nipples with saliva and blew on them until they stood out like perky little buttons… Where the hell did she pick that up? Maybe she saw it in a pornographic movie that I once brought home. Although she had made out as if she wasn't looking, she might have taken a peek. Now she was dancing like she had never danced before, her eyes closed, moving with herself, to herself, caressing her body, slipping one hand down her belly to her half unzipped jeans, cupping her swelling pussy. She started rubbing herself there, slowly, as if in a dream. I felt like a peeping Tom.

When I couldn't take it anymore, I unzipped my pants, whipped out my painfully taut dick and started masturbating with her, calibrating my hand to match her movements. She sat on the armchair with her legs apart. Her pink shiny pussy was wide open right in front of me. I could see its fluids dripping down her finger. She rubbed her clit and every now and then inserted a finger into her steaming hole. I could see she was about to come and I wanted to prolong my pleasure for just a few more moments so we could come together, but I was so horny I just couldn't hold it anymore. I exploded in such sweet relief that I kept my eyes closed for a while longer to hide the telltale moisture that forms in the corners when I come. When I opened my eyes, she was about to come herself, her mouth half open, her eyes shut, her breathing heavy and rapid. Then came the scream…. Oh my God how she screamed! They must have heard her scream all the way down to the lobby. Her sweet ass elevated for a moment and then, exhausted, her body collapsed like a limp cotton doll.

I went over to hug her, to tell her how amazingly beautiful she was. I took her to bed and started kissing her slowly, covering every inch of that sweeter than sweet body, the body I've known for fifteen years and that still excites me every time she takes her clothes off. I kissed her silky, white belly, making my way slowly but deliberately south. She doesn't always let me go down on her, and if she does it's only after a good shower, but this time she didn't say anything. She just ran her fingers through my hair. I spread the swollen, red lips of her pussy and tasted her. Her unique taste was delectable. I felt my dick rearing its head again. I started licking her slowly and thoroughly, every now and then leaving her clit in favor of her alluring hole, moving my tongue along its rim, round and round. Then I inserted my finger into her vagina, looking for that slightly swollen, lightly rough spot that is so distinct from the smooth walls around it. I knew how to make her come. It was as easy as pushing a button. I just had to press my finger upward and forward, thus adding double pressure to her clit, which was under heavy assault from my tongue. She twitched, clearly on the verge of coming and then came undone when I stuck another finger up her ass, which I know she loves. My Oh my, she flew high. Her sighs were music to my ears. I turned down the TV so I could hear her better. I really wanted to see her face but I was on duty in her heated pussy. Finally she came, even harder than before!

I waited for the earthquakes to subside before lifting my head. I could feel the electric currents that were convulsing through her body on my lips. It was a strange but exhilarating sensation. She smiled at me with eyes half closed from passion and pleasure. I rose to kiss her parted lips without stopping for a minute my attentive care of her pussy. I felt her pushing herself hard against my hand until I could contain myself no longer. She was having the best ride of her life and I was dying... I felt like if I waited one more minute, I'd faint from craving. I simply had to impale her, there and then, to fuck her to kingdom come, fuck her senseless, fuck her screaming and fuck her speechless. It was like a force of nature overcoming me, bigger than both of us. I lifted myself until the head of my dick was right at the opening of her pussy. I rubbed myself against her a little, teasing her. She loves it when I go inside just a bit and then go out again. Sometimes it takes a while until she opens up to me, but this time she was so wet, so ready for me, that she spread her legs wide and directed my vibrating rocket to the right place. I placed myself at the opening of her vagina and in one strong shove I dunked my dick inside her in its entirety. She let out a scream of intense pleasure and lifted her pelvis to me so I could fuck her harder and harder.

She just couldn't get enough... it was the best fuck we'd ever had. We climaxed together, howling like bears in heat, and this time she didn't push me immediately aside, like she usually does, but wrapped her long legs around me, squeezing her thighs together so I wouldn't leave her and said softly, "Let's stay like this a little longer, my love." I hugged her, looked deeply into her tear brimmed eyes and thought that she was more beautiful and more carefree than I'd ever seen her. At that moment I loved her so much that my heart exploded like a forty-kilogram dynamite charge and I felt myself melting, just melting inside.

For the four days in Rome we didn't stop fucking like a couple on their honeymoon. We planned the day so we'd get to the hotel for lunch, have a light meal and a fuck, and at night we had at least two rounds. It was amazing. My poor dick was chafed from being overused! Suddenly I had this disturbing thought that maybe we were setting standards we wouldn't be able to live up to when we got home. It goes without saying that when you're on holiday and have nothing on your mind, no pressures of work or children to care for, everything is so exciting and new, including your wife, you can get it up even when you're exhausted from sightseeing all day. But what if she got used to this and demanded the same level of performance at home? It bothered me a little, like the buzzing of an annoying insect, but I tried to drive the thought out of my head so as to not spoil the short time we had left in Rome.

When we got back home I had to put in a lot of

overtime in order to finish all the work that had piled up in my absence. All the tasks I had assigned to Itzik and Michal hadn't been done and there had been a serious delay in the processing of orders, which affected production. It meant staying at the office late. I came home around ten, or eleven o'clock, totally wiped out. The kids were asleep by then and Dina, although sometimes still up and waiting for me, was very tired herself. So it was for two weeks, then she got her period.

Afterwards one of my brothers came to visit. With everything that was going on, by the end of the month we had had sex only twice, and both times were quickies in the middle of the night when we were both very tired and she was doing me a favor so I'd sleep better.

One morning Eitan came into my office for a cup of coffee. We started chatting about the problems with the crops and the impressive performance of the new, expensive tractor, when he suddenly blurted out, "You brought a lot of problems with you from Rome when you bought Dina that book."

I gave him a sharp look, amazed that he knew anything about the special book that had become a part of my intimate relationship with my wife. "What do you mean exactly? How do you even know about this book?"

"Oh come on," he waved his hand dismissively, "this book has been going around to all the girls on the

Kibbutz for a whole month! They've all got the hots for it and are fighting about who gets it next."

I cringed as if he had just punched me in the kidneys. I felt as if the whole Kibbutz had just walked in on me and Dina in the middle of sex and seen us naked. The book, which had given us such exciting moments and had been part of our unforgettable lovemaking in Rome had now become the masturbation sex toy of the women of the Kibbutz. They were probably all talking about it, gossiping about Dina and me, picturing us looking at it and doing what we were doing in Rome. I should never have bought her the book in the first place! What an idiot! I should have warned her to keep it absolutely private. Now she has made a complete fool of herself, of both of us. I thought it must be Mirale, that blabber mouth, who had interrogated her about our vacation in Rome, and Dina, in her naiveté, must have told her everything. From there it had probably gone downhill to become the talk of the day for all the gossiping hens in the kitchen, the dining hall, the laundry and the secretary's office.

I couldn't hide the sour look on my face from Eitan and I saw a sly smile forming at the corners of his mouth. "Don't tell me you didn't know…"
I tried putting on the most complacent and nonchalant

face and said cynically, "I'm glad our book has been a source of entertainment for the girls on the Kibbutz."

Eitan chuckled in manly brotherhood, leaned closer to me and with a meaningful wink said in a low voice, "You'll be interested to know what Noa has done with it… given herself a hand job! I never thought that girls do it too but Mirale swears she wasn't making it up."

At this point I felt a little nauseated. If the book was in that bimbo's clutches then that was the end of it. The whole country, including my elderly second cousins in Dimona would hear everything about it, including the interesting fact that we bought it.

I resorted to sarcasm. "Really? Who would have thought that girls are human too?" But Eitan, a typical phalach (field worker) didn't understand the nuances of sarcasm.

"So…? Did you and Mirale also enjoy the book?" The question escaped my lips in spite of my aversion to gossip.

"What?" He seemed embarrassed. "No, not me, it's mainly Mirale. She confessed to me that she looked in the book and had a fantasy about some of the guys in there. You know, between you and me, I got curious, so I leafed through it, casual like. What can I tell you? I wasn't impressed. There wasn't anyone who was, you know, endowed really seriously, no one that you can look at and say, 'Oh, look at the cannon he's packing.' They were all completely regular, nothing you don't see every day in the showers on reserve duty."

I took my time aiming my arrow. "So, you're checking out the guys in the shower?" I shot him right between the eyes.

The smirk on his face froze and became a frightened giggle. "Me?! C'mon, you don't have to make a big deal out of it. I was merely making an observation."

At this point I was fed up with the whole thing and especially with Eitan, so I told him I had a meeting soon and I needed to prepare some papers. He got up quickly and said goodbye with what sounded like a sigh of relief. After he was gone I stared at the papers in front of me but I couldn't read anything. After some futile attempts I reminded myself about the imminent meeting with one of our most important customers and forced myself to drive the disturbing thoughts of Dina and the book out of my head.

While I was running around taking care of the business in the factory, I hardly thought of it. However, during breaks, during my turn at the dish washing machine after supper, or late at night when I was dead tired, I couldn't sleep because the bad thoughts, like a swarm of hornets, were circling in my head. At supper I sat in the dining hall with Dina and the kids and imagined people giving me strange looks or hiding their knowing smirks. It was a nightmare, and what made it worse was that Dina couldn't understand why I was mad at her for loaning the book to Mirale.

"But she promised to take good care of it," she said in a defensive tone.

"That's not the issue," I tried to explain. "Our intimacy has been compromised. This Kibbutz has been breathing down my neck for years. Everybody here has known us since we were twelve years old and now they're coming to bed with us as well."

"But sweetie, I look around and I see only you and me here."

I knew she was only trying to calm me down but it only made me angrier. Not only had she caused such damage to our relationship without even realizing it, but now she was also making light of my feelings and the situation, and it was driving me crazy. The more I tried to explain myself, the worse it got. She kept insisting that it wasn't as bad as I made it sound.

"Do you think we don't talk about sex when we get together? Of course we do! We enjoy talking about it as much as you guys do. But it's just girl talk. So what's the difference if it's only talk or if they also look at pictures that make them feel horny and talk about that?"

I felt she had barricaded herself behind the walls of her own point of view and she wasn't making the smallest effort to look at it from mine. We ended up having a huge and ugly fight, a very rare thing in our marriage.

Our sex life never really recovered from that fight. Whenever we started something I did everything mechanically, trying to shut out the bad thoughts for long enough to let me come. Sometimes I couldn't even do that. I felt like we were fucking with the windows open and the lights on, and all of the Kibbutz members standing outside watching us. Dina didn't say anything, but I knew she wasn't really enjoying herself either. It was clear she was only putting up with the sex for me. And that pissed me off even more. Before I was only looking for opportunities to be alone with my beautiful wife, but now I started passing up opportunities, even avoiding them. Dina tried a few times to drop hints, to say that now the kids were asleep and it was time for some grown-up activities, but I was so engrossed with my anger that I just couldn't welcome her attempts for intimacy. Finally she gave up and stopped trying.

That was another evil omen in my eyes. Why had she given up on us so quickly? She was usually quite determined when she wanted something. She isn't the type to shout and make a scene, but when she persists in nagging me with her calm determination, I usually cave in. So it made me think that perhaps there was something worse, much worse behind her silence, even worse than what the kibbutz members were thinking and saying of me. My Dina has always been so naïve;

you could say I've taught her everything she knows about sex. We were both virgins when we first made love, but being the man, of course my knowledge was far more extensive than hers. From the beginning she let me lead and counted on me for everything. I took it very slow with her. I knew that as a virgin she mustn't be hurried. She had to feel sexually aroused and want it herself, otherwise she'd be dry and frozen with fear, and we would both suffer.

It took her a long time, really long, to get to the point where she started cooperating. Sometimes I thought I would go crazy but I contained my frustration and tried to think of her, how she must feel, how frightened she must be and how painful it was for her. She maintained her silence but gradually her body began to tell me she was beginning to enjoy herself. She lifted her pelvis to me, guided my hand to places she wanted me to caress and when she was really having a good time she made these cute little sounds that melted my heart.

We've had a healthy, satisfying relationship all these years, we were so good together in bed, but for years she wouldn't tell me what gave her pleasure, she was that shy. Then suddenly, she picks up all these novel things like the strip-dancing? I don't know from where. Before Rome, when I came up with suggestions for sexual experiments she wouldn't hear of it, although I begged her! So how come she suddenly takes the initiative, orchestrating the scene, telling me what to do and how to do it? Where did all these lewd movements come from? Who taught her those tricks that would raise any man's cannon in no time?

The conclusion was inevitable. The stronger I tried to fight it, to erase it from my mind, evict it forcefully, the more it took hold of my thoughts and created a bunker I couldn't break down. It was the most terrible thought a married man could conceive. She must have another man. While I was running around like crazy, trying to do everything at work and at home so I could organize the vacation she wanted so badly, she could have easily had an affair right under my nose and I wouldn't have known a thing..

There were other voices in my head trying to plead for Dina, telling me this couldn't be the truth. The way she acted in Rome, like a bride on her honeymoon, how in love we were, she couldn't act like that and keep another man on the side. Dina doesn't know how to lie. She blushes deeply when she's hiding something. No. I've got to push this terrible thought out of my head. It just doesn't make sense. Come on, be sensible, I reprimanded myself. You're only torturing yourself as well as her. If she really had someone else you'd have seen the signs… something suspicious. And one of the "good souls" on the Kibbutz would surely have come to tell me. You can't hide these things, not on a Kibbutz.

I talked to myself incessantly, recruiting all the skills I needed to be as the brilliant marketing manager and negotiator I am. I tried to explain, to reason, to convince myself, but all in vain. Nothing helped. Nada. These crazy thoughts kept haunting me like a cloud of gnats was swarming around my head, making me jump, hop and dance, even try to outrun my dog in order to escape; but they follow me in hot pursuit, they're all around me, in my ears and up my nose, and I can't shake them off for a minute. This horrible buzzing sound is stirring up my brain and I think I'm going to flip in a minute.

Our relationship is like a fully loaded semi-trailer going downhill with broken breaks. The abyss between us grows daily. Suddenly I'm not sure if we'll ever be able to bridge the gap again. The silences between us grow longer. They are not silences of the good, consoling, heart-warming silence of cuddling in front of a good movie on the TV or going for a walk around the kibbutz in the cool night air, breathing the silent night into our lungs, listening to the frogs and crickets around the swimming pool, and the occasional howl of a jackal in the wadi. Only now, bad silences spread between us, creating an ever growing distance. She seems so far away that even if I scream I doubt she'd hear me.

We hardly have sex, and when we do it's like it's not me there on the bed with her, but somebody else, a complete stranger is making love to my wife while I'm standing in the corner of the room watching. I can see his unshaved cheeks scratching her. He hasn't shaved for a few days to spite her, because he knows she likes it when he is clean-shaven. He hopes she'll say something, get angry, yell at him, maybe hit him, but she just bites her lower lip and doesn't say anything. He passes a heavy hand on her breasts, not even trying to pretend to caress her, then flips her over and penetrates her from behind. She moans lightly and he rams himself against her tight ass, enraged, fighting against the knowledge that his erection is waning.

I'm suddenly watching Dina with all the men I decide she has slept with. Moshe, the hired cook, who made her something special every day; Dino the electrician, who came to fix our boiler and was caught watching Dina more than the dial for the hot water; Yedidya from the folk dancing course, who wanted to dance Polka and Krakoviak with her, swirling her in his arms at a tempo that made her dress fly up; Ziv, the male nanny in the kindergarten – I saw how he looked at her when we went to pick the girls up at four o'clock. They are all standing there, beside me, more me behind them, men whose faces are blurred, a long line of men standing in two rows by the side of the bed, making remarks about my technique and my private anatomy.

"Not bad, not bad, I'd give him an 80."

"What are you talking about?! He sucks at it!"

"I wouldn't go that far, but there's certainly room for improvement."

"Ah, I knew him when he was young. He was much better then."

"Look at the vigorous pelvis movements... he's bound to hurt his back in a minute."

"I'd give him six, tops."

"Out of hundred?"

"Out of ten! Ha ha ha."

"It's a pity his wiener is just a sausage."

"Oh-oh, he's losing power."

"The flag has gone to half-mast."

That poor, sweating guy on the bed... of course he can't climax with all these rude intrusions.

This bizarre scene taking place in my mind freaks me out completely. Dina notices my anxiety and tries to talk to me about it, but what can I tell her? That I can't fuck her anymore because in my crowded mind it has become an orgy? She'll think I'm crazy, and frankly, right now, I'm not so sure I'm not. Crazy, I mean.

I've got to talk to someone about it, before I lose my mind. But who can I talk to? It can't be anyone on the kibbutz, that's for sure. That's the last thing I need, to throw them another hot item for more gossip. What about Amos? I haven't heard from him in ages. We're always too busy to meet but when we do finally get together it always seems like just yesterday that we were in the Gar'in (a group of youth of who go together to the Kibbutz) together, living in that dilapidated shack at the end of the bachelors' hood with Shmil, hanging out on the squeaking swing on the summer nights, eating whole packs of sunflower seeds. I remember the famous, never-ending backgammon tournament, where Shmil was in charge of keeping the score charts, and they just got longer and longer, spreading over a few pages. We decided not to end the tournament before the whole notebook was full, but in the end the notebook got wet when the hot water boiler exploded and flooded the shack. Our tournament ended, but throughout the army service in the air force, as pilots in training, we continued to argue about who had more points. Shmil and I didn't finish the pilot training course and were moved to the armored corps but Amos finished. He was the only one from our Gar'in who made it.

I decide to call Amos and set up a meeting with him in Tel-Aviv, near his office. If he wonders about the nature of my urgent request, he keeps it to himself. It's good to see him but I find it difficult to start talking about the reason I've called him so we go through the whole list of small talk topics – family, work, a little politics and the ups and down of the stock exchange market. After about half an hour he takes a hard look at me and asks with his typical directness, "O.K., Yisrael, cut to the chase. You didn't bring me here after two years to talk about the stock market. What's going on?"

I open my mouth and then close it again.

He nods his head and says, "So it's about Dina."

That's the way it is with old friends. I don't see him for years but he understands me better than the people I live with and see every day on the Kibbutz. So I tell him everything. I try not to sugar coat the situation, not to hide or omit anything. I hate lies and cover-ups. I hate them in other people and I'm not willing to tolerate any in myself. When I screw up, I'm willing to take full responsibility. I even tell Amos that I don't blame her for the lousy situation we've found ourselves in, although, technically, it was her fault to begin with. After all she was the one who gave the book to her horny friends who then started passing it from hand to hand until the whole Kibbutz was in on the matter. I stare gloomily at the bottom of my beer glass.

"What's worse is she doesn't even understand why it made me mad. But everything that has happened since has definitely been my fault. I know I'm in a tailspin but I can't seem to stop my airplane from going down. Why do you think I called you? Please tell me how I can get out of this, and you'd better hurry because I've completely lost control of my plane and I'm about to crash. If we go on like this she's bound to ask me for a divorce, if she hasn't already started thinking about it."

Amos is silent for a long minute and then says slightly hesitantly, "Sorry, pal, I can't get you out of this one. The only one who can get you out of this tailspin is yourself. You have to pull yourself together, get a grip on yourself and do what you have to do. Right now you're in a dangerous situation that can easily end in a horrible crash but the good news is that it's not so difficult to get out of it. All you have to do is grab the steering wheel and hold on tight, real tight, until you come out of it. I don't think you've done that. You sort of let go."

I'm taken aback a little by his blunt answer. "Don't you see I can't do it? I don't know how!"

"I do see, Yisrael, believe me I do, otherwise you wouldn't be here talking to me. But what I see that you're talking to the wrong person. The one you should be talking to about this is Dina. You should tell her everything you've just told me."

"But how can I?" I burst out, frustrated. She will probably think I'm losing my mind, something I'm beginning to think myself."

Amos looks at me from across the table with his

typical calm expression, which this time, annoys me more than ever.

"If you ask me, I think she's already convinced you've lost your mind. When was the last time you took a hard look at yourself in the mirror? According to what you told me, you've been behaving strange for weeks now, very unlike your usual self. You two have grown apart. You spend all your time at work and don't come home until late at night, you don't make love to her, you respond rudely when she attempts to get close to you and what's worse – you won't talk to her about what you're going through! I'm willing to bet you a thousand shekels that she thinks either you're having an affair or you've gone stark raving mad."

I stare at him speechless. My stomach turns and cold sweat covers me. I can taste the nauseating bitter truth in his level-headed, icy, yet sensible words. I feel as if he's taken the binoculars I've been looking through and turned them around. Suddenly all the imaginary humiliation, the hinted insults, all the disturbing thoughts that have been buzzing around in my head seem so petty, almost absurd and insignificant compared to the grievous hurt I have singlehandedly caused to my marriage, and to Dina. Why couldn't I see it before? She must be seething, boiling mad at me, if she doesn't utterly hate me by now. What a fool I've been! To treat the woman I love more than anything in this abhorrent way!

Amos pours me another glass of beer and pushes it towards me. "Ahhem," he nods sympathetically. "It's a pretty shocking revelation to find out what an idiot you've been."

Judging from the angry honking behind me, I must be driving too slow but I don't care. Thoughts are swirling around in my head. I realize I have to act and act now if I want to save my marriage. I have to tell Dina everything, including the fact that she has married an idiot. On the other hand, the good news is that the idiot in question has finally come to his senses and is begging her to forgive him for the nightmare he has put her through. Could she please attribute it to temporary insanity brought on by misplaced jealousy?

When I get home we don't have time to talk. Every day this week I try to get home early in the evening to play with the kids, do homework with them and help Dina with supper. I even wash the dishes. I think she takes note of my efforts because every now and then she gives me a weird look, but only on the weekend do we finally have a chance to talk.

Finally Shabbat comes and it's a quiet one. We're neither expecting any visitors nor are we invited anywhere. I lie half awake, staring at the ceiling. Dina is still asleep. She is lying on her side, her face harbored in my shoulder, her warm breath against my skin. I examine different ways of starting the conversation and after a while I feel her stretching, making these funny little sounds indicating that she is waking up. I seize the moment when she arches her back and pass my arm under her waist, drawing her in for a close hug. "Good morning sweetheart," I whisper into her soft hair.

She raises her head to me, a wondering expression in her still-red eyes. I kiss her lightly on her lips and say emphatically, "Good morning, my wife."

"Good morning, dear husband of mine," she answers, taking her time with the words as if weighing them one by one. She keeps looking at me, her forehead wrinkled. "I didn't hear the spaceship," she says at last. "It must have come some time during the night. Did you come to Earth to replace that grumpy porcupine that has been living here for the past two months?"

I smile but a dart of pain pierces my heart. "I know I've been acting kind of strange lately, and it must have been hard on you, bearing with me. I can't tell you how sorry I am. I was sucked into a vortex of bad thoughts about the members on the kibbutz, who always gossip, and also about you. It drove me crazy. I knew I was in a bad place but I just couldn't stop it."

"What bad thoughts did you have about me?" she asks with a hint of anger in her voice.

"Ahmmm…" I try to buy some time to think how to get out of it but she doesn't let me change the subject.

"Yes?" She raises an eyebrow.

I lower my eyes and spit the words out quickly. "I thought you had another man."

She jumps and sits up in bed, her eyes popping with rage. "You," she talks very slowly now, ominously slowly, "in your sick jealousy, dared to imagine me with another man? And that's why you've been treating me like a stranger all this time?! Like someone you can barely tolerate?"

I see her eyes brimming with tears and my heart sinks. I reach out to wipe her eyes and repeat again and again, "I know, I know, you don't need to tell me what a complete idiot I've been. I tried to reason with myself but these evil thoughts kept poisoning my mind and I was too weak to stop them."

She exhales furiously. "I always told you that your jealousy will be the end of us. It has become insufferable. All the girls envied me for the amazing sandwiches that Moshe, the cook, used to make me, but I couldn't take them because I knew it would freak you out, so I had to give them away. In folk dancing I can never dance with a male partner who can spin me and lift me up properly. I have to make do with Mirale who does her best, but you can't expect her to lift me up, can you? And why do I give up all those things? Only because I know you're watching me and I immediately think what it's going to do you, how it's going to make you jealous, and I start thinking about the fits you're going to throw at home. I just can't take it anymore. But with all your jealous fits you've never gone so far as to actually accuse me of having an affair! Do you understand how ridiculous you sound, how disconnected from reality, how annoying, how insulting, how...?"

Her voice is broken by sobs while her face is buried in her hands. She is sitting in bed, her shuddering back turned to me. I want to bury myself ten feet under. I can no longer allow myself to deny the grave results of my actions. Filled with remorse, I caress her hair and stammer, "You're right. . I don't know, I didn't know, I couldn't stop myself. I can see now how absurd and destructive my jealousy has been. Please, Dina, I don't want to lose you. You and the children are everything to me."

She lifts her tear-stained face to me and spreads her hands in a gesture of utter amazement. "But why didn't you say anything? Why didn't you tell me? I would have told you outright that there never has and there never will be another man for me but you."

I gather all my courage and hug her tight, breathing in the familiar scent of her hair. "Just tell me I haven't wrecked our marriage beyond repair. Do you think you can find it in your kind heart to forgive me? Now that the grumpy old porcupine who has been your husband these past weeks is finally gone forever, and I promise you he'll never return, can you take me as you loving husband instead of him?"

She tightens her arms around me in response to my bear hug. I try to kiss her but she buries her face in my chest. I feel her tears dampening my chest hair. Her voice is broken and muffled.

"What I don't understand is how you fell into that dark pit of jealousy and sick, destructive thoughts right after we came back from Rome! For me it was our second honeymoon, even more beautiful and exciting than our first one! Every moment was so romantic and filled with passionate love. I was high, up in the clouds, I was so happy. I just couldn't believe how wonderful and exciting our relationship had become, like we'd just met. I don't think there are many couples who can reach such heights of love and passion after fifteen years of marriage. When we were there, drunk on erotic pleasures, I really thought it was too bad we hadn't done it before.

"We let ourselves get swept up by a smothering routine. And the children, you know how much I love them, but sometimes I'd like them to leave me alone for a while so we can be together as a couple. I was so happy we were finally living what we had planned and talked about for such a long time, and it really exceeded all my expectations. I kept thinking how now, after this second honeymoon, we wouldn't let our relationship deteriorate again when we got back, how we'd schedule 'dates,' maybe go to a romantic B&B cabin in the Galilee, or even a hotel in Tel-Aviv. Why not? We could explore the nightlife of the big city, go wild, just the two of us, like we used to… So tell me, how did you get from there – from the height of romantic love, our love – to that black pit of misery you've flung us both into?"

Her words pierce me like red hot needles. I suddenly realize how low I've sunk and it makes me dizzy. I know she expects an answer. I open and close my mouth like a fish out of water but the words just don't come out. What can I say that won't sound like a shallow excuse? I have to be totally honest with her and myself. That's the only thing that will save my marriage.

"I don't know," I confess. "Maybe it's because the height of passion we reached in Rome, maybe it's because I felt exactly like you. It was so good… too good to be true. We were not in our usual environment. We carefree, with no worries, of course we were happy. But it couldn't last any longer than a short vacation. The reality of life isn't like that, you see?"

She tightens her arms around me until I can hardly breathe. "No. I don't see," she says dismayed. "Why can't it be all good? If we love each other, and everything is so wonderful between us, why can't we just carry on like that? Is there some sort of cosmic rule I'm unaware of? One that says people can never be truly happy?"

I take a moment and a few deep breaths to ponder her words. Why can't I just be happy? Have I made up this cosmic rule that doesn't allow me to enjoy all the good things in my life? Seriously, why? I try to locate the numbness in my lower abdomen. It's a cold serpentine pain that crawls upward to my heart, always a second after a moment of elation, like after the successful completion of a great deal, or the height of love and passion we experienced in Rome. I know this pain. I've met it face to face a few times before. It's the same pain that made me leave the festive dinner party for my appointment as the factory manager, but it also feels like something else… like the pang of panic I managed to suppress when I saw the Hezbollah fighters coming toward us and I realized we were about to engage them in a face to face combat. I was paralyzed for a minute and my stomach convulsed with cold pain… It's fear! That's what it is! OMG, me, afraid? Yisrael, the strong, courageous regiment commander that the soldiers looked up to, that Dina could always depend upon and count on for help, afraid? No, it's not like me.

I protest silently against the vision I see reflected in myself. The memories of moments when I felt that cold fear crawling up from my lower abdomen, up my spine and to my heart, the fear that paralyzed me in the most beautiful, most moving moments of my life because of… Why? What was it? What was I afraid of? Of losing all the good things I have? I'm going to lose them anyway because of this fear. I've brought this on myself. Me, who has fought in many battles and won, am losing this one, probably the most important battle of my life. This was the most shocking part of that painful truth Amos that Amos was talking about.

Dina has grown tired of my long silence. She raises her eyes which are still red from crying and asks softly, "What is it, darling? What's going on in that dark and twisted mind of yours?"

I bite my lips and let the shameful truth escape from my reluctant lips. "I think I'm just… scared."
To my relief she doesn't make light of my confession by consoling me with, 'No way,' or something of the sort. Instead she ponders for a moment and asks me directly, "What are you afraid of?"

"I don't know. I can't put my finger on it… maybe it's a fear of the fall that inevitably follows every summit. Does it make sense? After all, you can't always stay on the top, you must come down sometime."

"Maybe yes and maybe no," she says thoughtfully, "but one thing is certain: after every descent there's always another climb up, another summit to reach, right? So you always have something to look forward to."

I look at her with a wondering doubt in my mind. This is it? It can't be that simple, can it? But then again – why not? All the best inventions are often the simplest ones, like the wheel. My head starts aching from all these psychological excavations. All I want to do is make up with Dina, and I'm trying to do that right now. "I hope you're right. I promise to think about it. But you still haven't answered me as to whether you'll take be back as your loving husband?"

She gives me a long, hard look that sends shivers down my spine. Her hair is disheveled, her eyes are red and there's a streak of dry tears on her cheeks, but she's still the most beautiful woman I've ever seen. Gradually her eyes soften, become warm and loving again and she hugs me, only this time it's relaxed, without the desperate anger.

We lie clinging to each other like two drowning people who have found a log at sea. We need some silent time to weave together the threads that have been torn between us. The emotional storm we've been through has left us totally exposed and vulnerable. My heart is about to explode with gratitude and joy that, in spite of everything, she still loves me.

Slowly, very slowly her belly starts rubbing against me and her pelvis performs a little salsa dance. It gets an immediate response from my attentive dick. I make a nonchalant observation: "Have you noticed the interesting fact that neither of us has dining-hall chores, we have no guests, and the children, for some unknown reason, are still fast asleep? Can you comprehend the ramifications of these interesting facts?"

"Ahmmm…" She purrs against my chest, "I think I know what you're up to, but tell me anyway. It turns me on to hear you say it."

"What do you think I'm up to?" I say with feigned innocence. "O.K., let's see… I intend to undress you and say good morning to your lovely tits…"

"It sounds good," she says playfully, "but I know you. You won't settle for such a simple scheme."

"You're absolutely right. You know me better than I know myself. From your tits I intend to move on to your soft belly…"

"Hey!" She protests. "Not so soft now that the new instructor in aerobics has been making us do all lots of abs exercises."

"Come on. Show me what you've got." Dina makes an effort to tighten her belly muscles. As a matter of fact, for a girl her muscular tonus isn't so bad. I tickle her until she bursts out laughing and has to let go. "Not bad," I say with an expert tone of voice, "but there's always room for improvement."

"O.K.," she concedes, "keep telling me about your plans."

"So from your belly I'll go down to your sweet pussy, so sweet that I can lick it for hours on end and never have enough…"

She closes her legs tight on my exploring hand and says expectantly, "Why don't you stop scheming and start acting on it?"

I get up to lock the door and she goes to the shower for a quick wash. When I turn around she is bending down and just about to wash her genitals.

"Allow me, my lady," I offer and she hands me the shower head, smiling. I kneel down so my head is right before her wet pussy. I spread its pink lips with one hand and with the other I point the warm current to her clit. From the sudden sigh that comes from above I gather that my aim is spot on, so I keep playing with the shower head, aiming it a little lower and then a little higher again, up and down, up and down over her beautiful temple of love. I'm turned on by seeing her wide open right before me like a flower in full bloom.

After a while I start using my fingers, rubbing her clit, pinching it lightly while simultaneously aiming the strong current of water so it hits her right on her sweet spot. Her sighs grow louder and louder. I insert my index finger into her vagina and point it upward while applying pressure on her clit with my thumb so it's right between them. Her legs start shaking in that familiar way and she leans on to me. When the shaking subsides I turn off the water, take a big towel and dry her thoroughly.

Her eyes are closed and there's a content smile on her face.

I kiss her and take her to bed where I take the towel off her naked body and start licking her slowly, from top to bottom. I can see the swollen lips of her pussy vibrating lightly, calling me to get back to them, but I take my time, nibbling her lightly along the waist line and on the insides of her thighs. When I finally get to her pussy again I take her outer lips between my fingers and massage them lightly while going around her pussy, crushing and rubbing, round and round, before I start licking her clit again. I hear her groaning into the pillow, and then she climaxes again and again until suddenly she pulls me up impatiently. "Come to me, my love, come to me now. I can't wait any longer."

Smiling, I hover above her, and slowly start sinking myself into her. Our eyes lock and there's so much love in them that for a minute I lose myself in regretting all the time we've lost when we were apart. How could I have misjudged her so? Damn it all – my stupid jealousy, the Roman book, her horny friends, the Kibbutz and the fear of what people might say. None of it matters anymore. It's just her and me and that electric current between us, a live wire that connects us to each other and to life itself. In this moment I feel like I can stay inside her forever, wrapped in her arms, our bodies intertwined so tightly. This second of orgasmic elation that unites our bodies and souls is the second I want to relive over and over again.